Cover Art:
MLC Designs 4U

Publisher's Note:

This is a work of fiction. All names, characters,
places, and events are the work of the author's
imagination.

Any resemblance to real persons, places, or events
is coincidental.

Solstice Publishing - www.solsticepublishing.com
Copyright 2015
Mel Massey

For you.

Prologue

Two covered figures, one bent with age and the other a child, quietly made their way from the main house into the night. The older of the two pulled the smaller one along in the dark by the hand as they walked further and further into the shadows.

This was the night of the new moon. It was the perfect chance to see the deed done. If what her son, Samir, told her was true, this would be the last chance she would have. She could not let her son and his family fall to ruin. She would not allow it. They thought her an old and feeble woman. True, the years have taken their toll on her body – but not her mind. Her mind was as keen as it ever was.

She remembered many things. Many lost and forgotten things handed down to her by her own grandmother. For many years, she had forgotten them all. Her marriage, her duties as a wife, and then motherhood whisked those tales away as if a hawk swooped down and carried them off. Only as she lay in her birthing bed, laboring to bring her sons into the world, did pieces of the tales return.

They gave her strength. She was a wife, mother, and now a grandmother – but once she was Luja who knew the family's secrets.

Now, after so many years had passed, she turned once again to those memories of her grandmother. The new moon was when one did this sort of thing, she remembered. Her granddaughter, Hala, was her ever-present shadow and she meant to share this thing with her. She pulled the sleepy child along in the dark, headed for the farthest corner of the gardens.

"I'm tired, Grandmother." Hala whispered.

"Hush, child. We have things to do, you and I." She looked once more over her shoulder and pushed on, past the unkempt and dying gardens to the farthest corner beside the stone wall. "I think this will do."

She handed Hala a small bundle wrapped in cloth before kneeling on the ground. She felt around until she found a stick big enough to suit her needs. With more force than she knew she still possessed, the old woman began to dig a hole beneath the olive tree. Her arthritic hands ached, but her spirit soared. She would see this thing done. It had to be done. No one else knew what she did. She would save her family.

Hala sat heavily on the ground, her head resting in her hands as she watched her grandmother dig. That was good. Let her see each step. Let her understand there are ways beyond those of the modern world to get what one needs. Tonight, she was herself again. She imagined herself the young and beautiful Luja who had a wild spirit and a quick temper. In the morning, she would be Grandmother again… but not yet.

Satisfied with the size of the hole, Luja reached for the bundle in Hala's arms. She snatched it from her and anxiously unwrapped the contents. The girl's curiosity roused her from her fatigue. She leaned forward to see the objects of the bundle laid out in the dirt. A precious bowl of honey and two figs sat beside another, longer item.

Luja carefully began unwrapping linen from around it. It was sacred to her family, her grandmother told her. It was only to be used in the direst of circumstances. How to use it was only taught to the daughters of the family, for men were not permitted to touch such things.

"What is that, Grandmother?" Hala whispered.

"Our salvation, sweet girl." From the folds of aged linen, a statue emerged. It was carefully made. The age, Luja did not know. She knew it was delicate and priceless. It was made from clay but held together by a thin layer of gold. It was the image of a woman, naked but for carvings on the body. She did not know what they meant but she showed Hala the statue reverently. It was as shiny as the day Luja's own grandmother showed it to her. She remembered her voice shook as she told Luja of the power in the statue and how it worked. Luja asked her grandmother if she would ever use it. "I would not dare," she told her. Well, Luja dared.

"Who is it? Why is she naked?"

"She is the one who will help our family." Luja told her.

"How? Papa says we have no money and soon we'll be living on the streets. Are we going to sell this, Grandmother? Sell it to pay the money Papa owes?" Hala's words drove a knife into her heart. No child should know of the woes of her parents. Samir was foolish and selfish to say such things where the children could hear. But his foolish and selfish ways were the reason they were in such dire straights. He gambled what they had and risked everything on dreams that never came true.

"No, my child. We will not sell her. She is priceless and too powerful to sell, but she can help us in other ways. Give me your hand," Luja carefully placed the golden statue in the hole and reached for Hala. "It will only hurt for a moment." Before the child could understand, Luja pulled a knife from the folds of her dress and made a small cut in the palm of her hand.

"Ouch, Grandmother!" Hala tried to pull her hand back but Luja kept it firmly grasped over the gold statue.

"She only requires a little blood, child. When you come of age, you will bleed every month. Blood is nothing to women. Men like to think they know of blood and pain but we are the ones who truly know. Now, you know the power of your blood. It is precious because you are a virgin, unspoiled by men. Mine would not do for this. There," she released her grip on the girl's hand and watched as the crimson droplets painted the gold surface. "That is enough."

"Who is she?" Hala asked, holding her injured hand close to her chest.

"She is the servant of the blood. She is the giver of desires and the force of the Mother. I do not know her name. She is what she has always been to our family – our salvation and our curse."

"What do we do now?"

"We bury her, Hala. Then leave the offerings. If they are pleasing, if we are pleasing, she will hear them and come to answer our prayers."

"Is it right what we are doing, Grandmother? I'm not sure Papa will approve," Hala said as she stood.

"Certainly, he wouldn't. If he did, I should question my actions."

"I don't understand–"

"Never you mind, my dear. Come, help me cover her and set these offerings to right."

"How will we know? How will we know if she will help us or not, Grandmother?" Hala asked as she scooped dirt back into the hole.

"I am not certain. We women must do what we can to save those we love. Here, hand me that bowl." Luja placed the bowl of honey directly above the buried statue. "There, we have done what we can. It is out of our hands now."

Luja and Hala covered their heads once again and silently made their way back through the garden toward the house. The girl still held her injured hand close to her chest and her grandmother pulled her along in the dark. It had been years since Luja felt so alive. She committed a great sin tonight. This sin was one she would not apologize for. She was a woman and women must do what they can in the shadows to see their families prosper in the light of day.

Chapter One

The fresh air filled her lungs and she gasped from the piercing pain of it. Smells of the earth filled her nose, mixed with new, more rancid smells that were unknown to her. Gagging and gasping for control, she rolled onto her side.

Her eyes blinked over and over again as her breath slowed and her eyes adjusted to the dark. She felt the dirt and debris that covered her body. Rubbing her hands back and forth on her arms, she finally felt her skin and smiled. She was alive.

Reclining back into the dirt, she surveyed her surroundings. She was in a small, earthen chamber. A cave perhaps? A hole deep in the ground? No matter. Wherever she was, it would not be long until she freed herself and walked once more among the living. She desperately wanted to hear music again. She wanted to dance to drums around a fire once more and feel the warmth of a man's hands on her skin. The delicious sensation of his eager mouth and able fingers caused flutters inside her. It was good to be alive and she would feel those sensations once more.

Slowly, she rolled over onto her side and raised her body from the ground. Her arms were weak. That would not do. Weakness would get her killed. Finding a way out of her dark hole was the first task to be sure. Feeling around in the dark with her hands, she found the mound of folded garments once placed beside her body. How long had it been? A very long time by the brittle feel of the mantle in her hands.

Her first attempt to wrap herself properly failed when the material fell to pieces. Many, many years must have passed since she was entombed in this place.

Her efforts to cover herself went only as far as wrapping a swath of material around her waist. It barely covered her womanhood. No matter. She would get what she needed in time.

She ran her hands across her breasts and felt the weight of them. Her hair had grown so terribly long in her years of entombment. She arranged long strands of black hair over her shoulders and felt the silken tendrils tickle her skin.

Standing carefully and feeling her way around the small room, she found the most important item she would need. Her dagger. It was beautiful with a blade that curved like the crescent moon. The handle was gold inlaid with a black diamond on the hilt. This must be used tonight, so she tucked it into her waistband and turned her attention to gaining her freedom.

After too long of a time, she finally decided she was in a cave. Everywhere she touched, rocks and dirt crumbled in her fingers. Although it was black as pitch, she closed her eyes and laid her head against the stone walls. The rocks, the womb of the Mother, kept her safe for so long. But now, now it was time for her to leave. She felt the call as she lay sleeping. It was a form of death but she could not die. Not a human death anyway. The call from her Masters echoed in her mind so loudly, she was aware even as she took her first breath. Now, the longing to go to her new master was overwhelming, yet, she remained trapped and weak.

She whispered into the darkness, "Show me the way…" Placing her hands on the rocks again, the cold stones felt exquisite on her cheek. She breathed in the smell of dirt and, for the first time, a mixture of salty air mingled with the other foreign odors. With eyes still closed, she followed the smell of the sea to the furthest wall from where she awoke. There, the air was cooler and she began to dig her fingers beneath rocks until they crumbled to her feet. One after another fell until she felt the entire wall give way.

She covered her head and face as a gust of fresh air enveloped her. Once more, she was born into the world from the womb of the Mother, eager to meet her new Master.

Stepping carefully over fallen rocks, she made her way into the night. The stars looked the same, if but a bit dimmer. She closed her eyes and smiled as the breeze carried familiar and unfamiliar odors to welcome her to this new age. How long had she been gone this time? She did not know. She had seen so many ages in her many lives. Once belonging to a tribe of nomadic people, all she saw were the desert sands. However, the Gods are cruel and take away what we love and take comfort in, only to hand us our unspoken fears as gifts and teach us to love them. That was the way of the Gods. Life and death. Gifts and curses.

Slowly, she made her way down the side of a mountain she found vaguely familiar. Every few steps she stopped and felt the invisible tug in the direction she needed to go. Turning to the more eastern side of the mountain, she realized she was headed for the cluster of lights down below. Small houses nestled against the side of the mountain, not far from the coast if the amount of salt in the air was true. More excited to be alive again rather than fearful for her fate, she made her way faster down the mountain.

An hour or more brought her feet to the ground in the dark. Her Master was not far away; she could feel the involuntary pull in that direction. However, one of her kind does not present herself to her new Master weak and void of power. She must complete that which was started with blood.

Still baring her breasts and enjoying the cool night air upon them, she walked quietly toward her goal. The sea was not as close as she first thought, she realized. Her feet felt the fertile ground beneath and she stopped to wiggle her toes into the rich earth. No. This was a farming city. Her eyes, now accustomed to the dark, saw the plants standing in perfect little rows like a proper army. Laughter escaped her mouth before she could stop it. How long since she had laughed? Too long. Throwing her head back, she laughed again. She laughed at the Gods for her new life. She laughed at herself for her fate. She laughed because she was alive.

The small houses were closer now and she needed to be quiet. She could hear the sounds of farm animals nestled together for the night. She would need to find the perfect one, one that would not disturb the animals in their rest. The beasts would get frightened by the smell of blood and wake everyone. That would not do.

She passed one flat house surrounded by farmlands. There were people inside, yes, but they were too large in number. She was too weak to take on such strength just now. Once this deed was done, she would be able to topple kingdoms and desolate armies. It had to be the perfect sacrifice. She would know it when she saw it.

Hours still lay ahead before the sun awakened. She walked barefoot and barely covered until she found a small house alone in the field. There were people inside, lost in their dreams, not knowing their nightmare walked toward them. Quietly, she approached the house from the shadows, each step measured and careful not to make too much noise.

Closer and closer she moved until she could feel their heartbeats as they lay sleeping. They slept in such innocence, such blissful ignorance to their doom that was now at hand. As she made her way to the back of the house, a new smell greeted her nose. Fire. Nothing smelled as rich and fine to her as a fire at night. Fire is an intoxicating blend of magic and power masquerading as warmth and light. Such fools humans turned out to be. She knew the last time they had all but forgotten their true roots. This age seemed to be even further away than the last.

Following the smell, she found herself watching a man coax a fire to life. He was huddled over it, blowing on the embers. He was a beautiful man, much like the men of her tribe so very long ago. His skin was bronze and his hair as dark as night. She knew her people by their eyes and the vibration of their soul. Yes, this was a good match for her. She watched his hands deftly arrange the wood in the pit until he was satisfied. She was torn between taking him as a lover or a sacrifice. Certainly, he would do as either but the irresistible tug cautioned her against tarrying too long. Taking a lover would have to wait.

She stepped from the shadows. It took the man a few moments before he realized she was standing there. The shock on his face would have made her laugh merrily if it were not the need for stealth. She watched as the man rose and rubbed his

18

eyes in a desperate attempt to see if she were a figment of his imagination. A smile spread across her face as the realization spread across his that she was indeed real.

"What are you doing? What are you doing here?" he whispered hoarsely. Still smiling, she stepped closer and brushed her hair back revealing her exposed breasts. She watched as his eyes drank her in. She knew he wanted her. His heart raced and he wrung his hands. He made to speak again as he tried to look over his shoulder but he could not tear his eyes from her. She stepped closer still and reached out for him.

She took his hand and brought it to her breast. His breath quickened, as did hers, when his warm skin touched hers. She sighed and placed a hand on his cheek. She wanted this man. It had been too long. As he squeezed her breast in one hand and reached out for her with the other, she fought with the desire to take him there under the stars. It would be quick, she knew. However, after so long, that would take far too much energy and she needed all that she had.

With a sad sigh and a longing that could not be sated, she reached to her side and freed her dagger from her waist.

"You are chosen," she whispered. He did not have a chance to reply. She plunged the dagger into his heart before the words fell from his lips. With shock still etched onto his face, he fell to his knees, hands trying in vain to stop the blood. He was dead in moments.

She rolled him onto his back and opened the loose garment he wore to reveal a tantalizing, masculine chest. Yes, he would have made a superb lover. His strength, and her sacrifice of such a specimen, would give her more pleasure than feeling him inside her. She sat astride his chest and plunged the dagger once more into his skin. She pulled the blade down, past the bones, and finally to the soft parts of his belly.

Placing the dagger back at her waist, she plunged her hands into the warm, wet inside of her beloved. She only needed one thing from him now. Her expert hands had done this many times and she felt the warm, hardened tissue that gave him life. It was always hard to remove it once it was firmly in her hands. Her hands were so small, the wet organ slipped from her grasp many times before she was able to tear it from its home. With wet noises she had heard many times before, his heart left his body.

Slowly, she turned the organ around in her hands, feeling the grooves and smooth tissue. She stuck a finger inside one of the tubes that once connected it to his body. It was still warm inside. That was always best; warm blood meant it was fresh and strong.

She brought her bloody finger to her mouth and traced her lips with the crimson blood. Now, his strength was hers. She left her would-be lover for the pitiful fire that had all but gone out. That would not do. With the wave of her hand, the pit roared with flames. She offered the heart up to the fire, watching as it shriveled and turned black. He was strong and she felt the power coming back to her as his heart was consumed. A warmth began in her own chest and spread to her belly. He would not be enough, though. She had been asleep too long.

She turned to the house and felt even more keenly those that slept within. She needed them. All of them. Once they were sacrificed, she would be at her full strength and her Master's call would be answered.

***

It did not take long to see the deed done. There was only an old woman, a young man, and two children inside. All of them died peacefully in their sleep. The blade slicing their necks so expertly all but one never even awoke. The young man tried to fight. He was strong and fought death gallantly. But death always wins. She watched the last of the light leave his eyes and admired his effort once he was still. Such spirit should not go unnoted. Once she took his heart, she posed his body like the warriors of old. She crossed his feet at the ankle and placed a small carving knife in his hands in place of a sword. That was a fitting tribute to such a young warrior. All young men dream of being warriors, but not many can be buried as such. He should be honored by her efforts.

By the time the sun brightened the sky, all that lay within were long dead and cold. Because of their fate, she was alive once more. As she made her way from the house, she decided to go by way of the fields and avoid the roads. Tucked under her arm were a few beautiful pieces of cloth that had belonged to the older woman. She thanked the woman once more for her sacrifice as she made her way to a runoff of a nearby lake. The water was cold and she needed to rid herself of the years of dirt and dried blood.

Soon she would be clean and new again. Once ready, she would meet her Master and see what the Gods had in store for her in this life. Lying naked in the water, she smiled up into the sun.

"I am Allatu. I am alive."

Chapter Two

Dinner was a somber affair for Luja's family that night. There hadn't been enough food for over a week and now their dinner consisted of only couscous, chorba, and dried olives. The last remaining figs disappeared mysteriously much to Samir's disappointment.

"This chorba tastes like water." Samir said as he poured a spoonful back into his bowl.

"Because it is mostly water, Samir," Luja said, never looking up from her bowl of broth. If they were a proper family, there would be delicious bits of lamb or fish floating in the herbs. Meat was not something they could afford any longer.

"I do not like it. I want something different," he exclaimed, pushing his bowl away, spilling the contents onto the table. His wife, Reshma, moved to wipe away the mess. He glowered in her direction as an uncomfortable silence settled over them all.

"I like it, Mother," Hala declared gleefully shoveling handfuls of couscous in her mouth. Luja smiled into her bowl and whispered another silent plea to her ancestors for aid. So much time had passed since she buried the statue. Should she dig the statue up and sell it as the child suggested? Was her sinful trip into the night the result of fairytales her grandmother told her?

"Why is there no fish? Is it too much to ask that a man be fed properly at his own table?" Samir raged on as his wife sat in stoic silence. Luja had never cared much for the cowering woman who married her son. However, the match made sense at the time. Still, her grandchildren were worth all of the heartache. The first born was Daayna. Now almost a woman herself, Daayna stood the best chance of escaping her father's ruin by marrying a man she had never met. It was a good match and Luja wanted her grandchildren safe. Jammana had only recently shed the look of a child and was welcoming womanhood beautifully. In a few years, she too would marry a man and Luja could not wait for that day. If only for Jammana's sake. Then there was young Aadil, who was a boy not yet ten, but following too close in his father's footsteps. If help did not come soon, Aadil's fate would be ruin and poverty. The youngest, and most dearly loved by all, was her precious Hala. The only child born to her son that carried her own spirit and will to live.

"You all are against me!" Samir raged on as everyone avoided his gaze. "After all I do for you… you ungrateful women know nothing, even about cooking a simple dinner." No one said a word, only Hala and Luja continued to eat on in silence.

"What was that noise?" Aadil asked.

"There is nothing left to cook—"

"I said I wanted fish, woman. You disgrace this house with this feeble slop that even a cow would not eat." He spat in her face. Reshma lowered her eyes and took the abuse. Later, Luja knew, she would endure even worse abuses once the children were asleep. Her son's arrogance did not allow him to blame himself, so he lashed out at the one by his side. The one he blamed for all of his misfortune.

"There it is again, Father. What is that noise?" Aadil asked softly. Samir was not listening. She could see the rage in him building up behind his dark eyes. Once they were kind eyes, so full of laughter and mischief. Now they showed only accusations and resentment.

"I hear it, too," Hala announced.

"Hush, Hala. Be quiet," Daayna whispered to her sister.

"But I do. It sounds like someone is walking around outside. Maybe we have a visitor. Grandmother, maybe it's—"

"Be quiet, child," Luja silenced her with a warning look. "Know when you should and should not speak." Hala's eyes dropped to her bowl and she nodded silently. Asking the young girl to keep their secret was a big thing, Luja knew, but women had many secrets. It was best she learned early how to keep them.

Samir was banging his hand on the table with each word, "You are not a good wife!"

Disgusted by her son, Luja turned away from the scene at the table and thought she, too, heard noises from outside. Leaning away from the table, she thought she caught a glimpse of someone in the shadows.

"Samir…" she said softly.

"I never wanted to be married, did you know that? I never wanted a wife but my father told me it was my duty to marry you!"

"Samir," Luja called out more forcefully.

"I knew when I saw you that you were not worthy of me. You did not deserve a husband like me."

"Samir!" Luja said with such force that the entire table turned to look at her. "The boy is right, there is someone outside. Best see who it is."

Samir slammed his fist on the table once more before walking away from all of them. Daayna attempted to comfort her mother and Luja strained to hear what happened with her son. She wanted to follow him, but it was not her place. He would deal with whoever it was. But before that thought was even finished, she heard her son yell.

"Should I go to Father?" Aadil asked.

"No child, you stay." Luja said as she left the table to join her son. She was afraid for him. Deep in her bones, she felt fear unlike any she had ever felt before. This fear transcended any other fear she could imagine. Impending doom and power vibrated in every cell in her body.

Luja left the family at the table and walked towards the door that led to the back gardens. Samir had left it open and she thought the noises were coming from the back terrace.

"Samir? Is everything alright?" she called out. *Please do not let anything happen to my son,* she begged silently.

"Mother... " she heard her son call out. His voice had changed. This was not the angry man from moments before, but an echo of her son from long ago when he was hurt and afraid.

"Samir... where are you? What has happened?" Luja stepped out into the night and saw her son huddled on the ground, cowering.

"It was you who called to me," Luja turned to see the outline of a woman in the shadows. "This man here says he is the master of this house. I did not come for the master of the house. I came for *my* master. That is you." Luja's hand covered her heart. She was too old to be this frightened of a woman in the shadows. There was something about the woman standing there that lit her soul on fire. She felt the primal connection immediately and then she understood. This was *her*.

"You came... you are really here." Her words fell to silence as the mysterious stranger stepped closer. The light from the house fell across the woman's face putting it in relief. She was beautiful, no doubting that. A fierce light was in her eyes made worse by the smile that slowly grew.

"Mother...what are you saying? You invited this... this whore here?" Samir seethed. Now that the attention was no longer on him, his fear turned back into rage and he stood, holding himself in a pompous stance.

"She is no whore, my son. I urge you to watch your tongue from now on," Luja said with a small smile of her own growing.

"Watch my…watch my tongue in my own house? How dare you?"

The woman did not move except for a flick of her hand and Samir lay in a crumpled heap feet away from where he stood moments before. Luja knew she should feel bad for her son, laid so low by a woman, no less, but she couldn't. Her faith in her grandmother and her tales were true. She would honor her own family for once.

"He is your son, Mistress?" the woman asked Luja.

"Yes," she sighed heavily. "That is my son, Samir." Hearing his name, he looked up into the face of the woman with defiance. "He is a good boy, underneath all of that posturing and hate." The woman stepped closer to Samir and leaned forward so as to have a better look at him. Luja saw the new addition to their family wore very little and flashes of flesh could be seen between the folds of cloth.

"I do not care for you, Samir, man of the house. The deepest parts of you have all but rotted away and all that is left is greed and vanity." Her voice rang out into the night as if this declaration was something to celebrate. "You are a most dangerous type of man. Made dangerous by your inability to be a man. It is a sad thing, to be sure. Lucky for you, your mother is a woman of depth and wisdom. She shall raise your family from this pitiful crypt you have placed them in."

"Do not be too hard on Samir. He is—"

"He is weak, Mistress. You would do well to replace him with another son. Do you have another?" The woman turned to Luja with her question. Luja's heart ached for the others lost to her and shook her head. "Hmm... that is not good news," she turned back to Samir who was shooting daggers at both women. "Then I shall try my best to transform you, Samir, man of the house. I shall see to it that you are worthy of me."

"Forgive me, do you have a name? What do I call you?" Luja asked wringing her hands. A part of heart leapt for joy at the mysterious woman's words and the other felt fear for what she saw in Samir's eyes.

"I do, Mistress. I am Allatu. Summoned by you to give you all that you desire."

"Mother, you did this? You brought this demon into my home—"

"Demon?" Allatu laughed. "I am no demon, Samir. I am a woman. The fiercest that has ever lived." Allatu tossed back her shoulders and smiled at Samir. There were shadows of mirth and violence in her smile.

"We better go inside before anyone sees. Come, let me show you our home." Luja motioned for Allatu to follow but Samir made a move to stop her. He grabbed Allatu by the arm and tried to pull her away. With a smile, Allatu grabbed Samir by the throat and lifted him, kicking and gurgling, into the air. Still smiling, Allatu looked back to her mistress.

"I could kill him now. It might better serve your family to mourn his passing instead of everyone's. For I speak the truth, sweet Mistress, he will bring ruin to you all."

"I know it, but he is my son and I cannot have him killed. We shall try and tame him." Luja said looking directly into her son's eyes. He held onto Allatu's wrists, trying to break her grip. His feet kicked out but she gave him a little shake to make him stop.

"Very well, Mistress. Nevertheless, remember my words to you. I shall make his passing quick and painless when the time comes."

Luja mumbled, "It isn't necessary," as she stepped inside with Allatu, still holding Samir's throat, in her wake. Cries of terror from the rest of the family greeted them as Allatu tossed Samir to the floor like an old toy.

"Grandmother! What is happening?"

"Is Father okay?"

"Who is she?"

"She's here!" Hala cried out. Allatu and the rest of the family turned to the youngest, smiling face. Only Luja and Allatu smiled back at her. Hala smiled from ear to ear and could barely contain her excitement. Allatu stepped forward regarding the child with mild interest.

"It was your blood that was used to wake me. For that, I thank you, little one. I hope to serve you in the future. But for now, because of your sacrifice, I shall grant you your very own wish," Allatu told the young girl. Hala smiled and screwed up her face, trying to decide on what she would ask.

"Do not ask this whore for anything. I forbid it!" Samir cried out. Hala's smile faded and her head dropped. Reshma reached out for her and tried to pull her away from Allatu.

"But... but, Father, Grandmother and I brought her here. She's going to help us. We don't have any money," Hala said to Allatu ignoring her family's cries. "We are hungry. Could you give us a proper dinner tonight? If we had good food, like father wanted, maybe you can stay?" Hala asked, squeezing her small fists in defiance of everything she knew.

"You are a brave little one. What name was given to you?"

"Hala."

"Hala. It is a pleasant name. Very well, Hala. I shall give you and your family a feast tonight. Then, after you are sated, we will speak. For I, too, am famished." She said the last part with a wink to Hala, who smiled. Allatu turned from the people in the room and raised both hands over her head. Luja saw her lips move but could not make out the words.

The front door opened with a bang that made everyone jump. A hard wind filled the house and made paper fly about and everyone cover their heads to avoid getting a smack in the face. Aadil ran to the table where they sat only minutes before expecting a miracle. He returned with a frown on his lovely face.

"There isn't any food. She lies." Samir stood, emboldened by the words of his young son.

"Out of my house this instant. We will not entertain your devilry any longer," Samir declared, pointing at the door.

"Hello?" Everyone turned to the newcomer who stood in the doorway. Luja knew him; he was Moazzam, the butcher. "I have your delivery here. Sorry. I seem to be running very late tonight." He motioned for the young boys who stood behind him to bring in their heavy burdens. One young boy entered and placed a wrapped side of lamb on the table, the next a sack of potatoes, tomatoes, and bunches of fresh herbs. The last boy brought in armfuls of bread and sausage. "I better leave you to it. I thank you for the prompt payment. Happy to see things turning around for you and your family." With a nod, Moazzam left.

A shocked silence filled the room before the chattering of the children took over. The girls looked over the food that sat on the table; even Aadil stared longingly at the sausages. Luja took over, barking out orders for everyone except Samir. The latter stood staring silently between his family and Allatu.

"I am not a demon, Samir," Allatu said quietly as she approached him. "But I am more than human. I serve the women of your family and have served them for far too many years to count. After we eat, you, my mistress, and I will plan the future of your family." Allatu was happy he had no response this time. She felt the battle in him to defy the woman before him and the greed for everything he had ever wanted. Which side would win, she could not say. If he became a threat to the family, she would remove him. The magic that woke her meant she was to do all that was necessary to elevate them—even if that meant removing the head of the house.

Chapter Three

It was a fine dinner, although terribly late into the night. Reshma had outdone herself preparing the food despite the mysterious arrival of Allatu. They ate mostly in silence, except for Hala, who chattered on about this and that. Luja barely paid the child any mind. She could not stop staring at the woman across from her.

Allatu was tall and lean. Her body showed no aging and, had Luja not known the truth, she would have said she was seventeen or eighteen years old. Her thick black hair hung in messy tangles that cascaded over her shoulders. The ends turned into lazy curls that brushed the back of her thighs. Her face was beyond beauty – no words seemed appropriate for a face such as hers. She could make any man fall instantly in love with her with a simple glance. Her laughter lifted Luja's spirits. Her eyes touched her soul. Reshma could not bear to look at the woman, nor could Daayna. But Aadil and Hala seemed quite at ease with the supernatural creature that shared their dinner.

Daayna and Jammana cleared the table as Reshma sent the two younger children to bed. Luja wished for *Ahwa Arbi,* her favorite after-dinner coffee. The days of drinking coffee had long since passed for this house. However, the realization that that might change brought a smile to her face.

"Have you no wine for me to drink?" Allatu asked as she showed herself the rest of the house.

"We do not drink in this house. It is forbidden." Samir said with a frown. Luja knew her son would escape to local bars and drink despite his posturing as a proper man. She held her tongue and waited for the shock to leave Allatu's pretty face.

"Forbidden? By whom?" She turned to Luja who pointed at her son. "That will not do. I require wine—and a lot of it. We shall see to that on the morrow."

"We will not see to that. This is a traditional house and we do not drink," Samir spat back to her.

"I am not a traditional woman, as you can see. I think it is time to tell you all. Sit." Allatu handed out the command as if she were a queen. Luja took her usual chair and Samir slowly lowered himself to the tattered sofa. Allatu paced the room fingering photos and picking up the worthless knickknacks Reshma collected. With a disgusted look, she turned to the two in the room and smiled.

"You called to me, Mistress, and I answered. Here I am. What do you know of me, Mistress? I need to make sure you know all before we continue. Mistakes cannot be made."

Luja cleared her throat, glanced at her son then back to the woman. "I know very little. Only that you are connected to my family and that you are the giver of desires, the servant of the blood."

"Yes. That is so. Blood of the sacrifices feed my power. With my power, I can elevate this... humble family to heights unseen. Where are we? Last I was laid to rest, it was in Tunisia."

"You are in Tunis, Allatu. Well, a bit outside of the city, but you are still in Tunisia."

"That is good. This was my home once... long ago. I prefer to stay here; however, I go where I must. Where my Masters send me."

"You have travelled much in your... your life?"

Allatu laughed merrily. "Oh yes, Mistress. I have travelled farther than I had ever dreamed I would. I have seen lands and peoples from all manner of histories. However, as I said, I prefer to be here in my homeland."

"Enough," Samir cut in. "I want to know what you will do for my family. There are things we need— now—in order to survive."

"Very well. I can give you anything you desire if my Mistress wishes it."

"Why her? Why not a man? I am head of this house," he demanded.

"As you have said many times this night." She smiled and tossed herself lazily onto the sofa beside him. "I am servant of the Mother. I serve only the women in this family. It is beyond my control that rule."

"Absurd," Samir mumbled.

"What are the rules, Allatu? Are you like a *Djinn*? Do you simply grant a few wishes? And at what cost?" Luja asked more interested in the history and lore than the present issues.

"My, my, Mistress. You are a shrewd one. No. I am not a *Djinn*. They grant wishes and twist them for one purpose or another. I am something else entirely. My purpose is to serve your family and see that you all prosper. I will do whatever is necessary to see it done."

"Whatever is necessary?" Luja asked quietly.

"Oh yes. Previous Masters have had me murder their rivals. Steal lovers from one another—but most simply want riches."

Samir's face lit up at the word. "Riches? You can do this?"

"Oh yes, Samir," Allatu smiled coyly and stretched out her long legs so they lay across his lap. "I can give you whatever your heart desires. Riches are easy to come by, if you know where to find them."

"So, you do not summon these things from thin air?" Luja asked waving her hands.

"No. I simply… redirect them from others. There is always a cause and effect in this world, My Lady. For one family to prosper, another must be laid to ruin."

"The world simply works that way," Samir said offhandedly.

"It does. However, I work in my own way. For every desire I fulfill of yours, you must fulfill one of mine." She gave Samir a deep look that made Luja blush and look away.

"What," he swallowed deeply before continuing. "What do you want?" he asked. Allatu laughed again, chasing away the warnings in Luja's heart.

"I am a simple creature, Samir. I said I wanted wine and I shall have it. If I am to begin to fill your family's coffers, I will require rooms of my very own and beautiful things within them. That will be a good start. The more you need, the more I will ask of you." She gave him a sly look and, Luja noted, Samir did not flinch from it.

"Seems reasonable," he muttered.

"Yes. I am very reasonable. Your family is in need of money, yes?" Samir and Luja nodded. "Very well. You shall receive money on the morrow."

"How much money?" Samir asked with greed in his eyes.

"As much as is needed to see your family fed and my needs met. If you want riches beyond count—that is a discussion for another night." She smiled and removed her legs from Samir's lap. "I will walk a bit through your gardens while you sleep. Go. Rest well. For tomorrow will hold many wonders for you." Her dismissal brought Samir to his feet. Luja stood slowly, noting the pain in her hips had returned. She watched as the strange, ethereal creature ventured outside into the night.

"I should scold you for this, Mother. I should. But I will forgive you your treachery because it seems things will start to improve soon. If what she says is true."

"I believe what she says is true. Take care my son," she turned him by his shoulders to face her. "Take care not to anger her too deeply. She is not a woman of this age. She is not even truly a woman, Samir. She is beholden to an age when magic ruled the world and her ways are not ours."

"She is beholden to us because of you, dear Mother," he kissed her forehead. "For that, her sins will be forgiven."

Luja watched him walk down the hall to his bedroom. He was an ignorant man. He thought he had some control over this. Even Luja, as Allatu's Mistress, knew in her heart the control she had was as fragile as a bird's wings.

***

"Mother," Luja heard Reshma's voice in the fog of sleep calling to her. "Mother, wake up. You must wake up." Luja opened her eyes, blinked a few times, then saw her daughter-in-law standing over her. "Are you awake?"

"I am now," Luja coughed as she struggled to sit upright. "What is it?"

"The woman, that wretched creature you brought here," Luja sighed. "She was walking around the house this morning with no clothes on! She has no morals! She has no decency!"

"Reshma my daughter, she is not like us. She does not see things the same way you and I do."

"I don't care, she's wicked. Wicked, I tell you. When I told her to cover herself, she laughed at me. She said the most cruel things…"

"Did she? Well, I will have words with her. I shall tell her to treat you more gently, is that what you want?"

"I want you to tell her to act with decency in my house! But that isn't the worst of it." Luja groaned as she pulled herself from her bed. She chuckled a bit thinking of what Reshma's face must have looked like upon seeing that naked beauty in her home.

"Help me, would you?" she extended her arm to Reshma who took it and helped hoist her upright.

"After she laughed at me, she demanded I bring you to her. Like I was a servant!" Reshma's voice reached a terrifying level of hysteria and Luja had to wrap her arm around her daughter-in-law.

"Calm yourself. It will take time to grow accustomed to her being here with us."

"She cannot stay, Mother. I forbid it."

"You forbid it? Hmm," Luja grabbed her favorite scarf for *Hijab*. Her hair was thinning and almost completely gray, no man would look upon her with desire in his eyes. But she was a slave to tradition, if nothing else.

"Yes, I forbid it. She, too, must wear proper clothing and stop… "

"Well? What else must she stop doing?"

"Looking at my husband, your son, with lust in her eyes." Reshma was still a beautiful woman. Had she proper clothing and perhaps a bit of makeup, she would still be a beauty. Her husband robbed her of those things.

"I shall speak to her. Let our guest know I will be down in a moment, if you please." Luja escorted her daughter-in-law to the door and closed it abruptly behind her. She placed a hand over her mouth to suppress her laughter. She knew she should be shamed by the laughter bubbling out of her now, but she simply wasn't. It was time to shake everyone from their dark thoughts and Allatu was just the one to do it. If anything, she would make Luja's remaining days on earth extremely entertaining.

***

It was quite entertaining to Luja to watch how many shades of red Reshma's face turned over a delicious cup of tea while Allatu chattered on about her desire for a lover.

"Do you not have friends that come to call on you? I should like a tall man with a broad chest. I do so like beards," she sighed and draped her leg over the arm of the chair in a terribly unladylike way. "Perhaps a party is in order!" Allatu exclaimed.

"That is impossible," Reshma said through clinched teeth.

"Nothing is impossible. If I want a party then a party I shall have." She popped a cube of sugar in her mouth and smiled as the sweet granules melted on her tongue.

"There will be no party! I will not—"

Allatu's voice cut her off. "There is the man of the house," she exclaimed with far too much enthusiasm than was decent.

"What are you doing sitting around? I sent Aadil to fetch your wine," Samir said the last word with a disgusted sneer. Allatu laughed merrily and clapped her hands like a child.

"Very good! We were only now discussing the need for a party here—"

"Party? Why do we need this? What good is a party for me?" Samir cut in.

Allatu's eyes narrowed. "I say we will throw a party," she rose from the chair, flicking her long hair over her shoulder. "If I say we need to throw a party, I have good reason to say this thing. Picture it, Samir." She wrapped her arm through his and pulled him closer to her resting one of her breasts on his forearm as she spoke. "All of the wealthy families meeting in your home. We shall offer them only the finest food and wine. Dancers will excite the men. The women will also have their own entertainment." She turned to wink at Luja, then faced Samir. Her dark eyes outlined in black charcoal were mesmerizing.

"I have already told her that it is impossible," Reshma said from the table as she watched the strange woman with her husband.

"It is important to announce your new position in the world with style, Samir. Your family

47

will rise with my help. A party is how you do this thing. You will be the envy of everyone for hundreds of miles. They will see how wealthy you have become."

"I suppose a party is not a bad idea."

"But Samir—"

"It will be lovely and you will rise to great heights. But we cannot have the party here." she looked around the small house and scrunched her nose in an oddly human gesture.

Samir looked around and spread his arms wide. "What would you have me do? This is my home and although you promised—" he pointed an accusing finger in her direction "—I have no money so this is all there is."

"Is it?" Allatu quipped. She smiled and flung the front door wide open. "I can smell the sea." She inhaled deeply and smiled a secret smile. "I wish to live closer to the sea. I wish to hear the waves crash and smell the salty ocean even in my dreams."

"Do you propose we move, my dear Allatu?" Luja asked. The prospect of leaving the farmhouse excited her. It would be good for the children to live where they could make friends, go to a good school and find proper spouses.

"Yes," she said breathlessly. "Yes. You shall leave this place."

"This is a family home. I will not part with it," Samir insisted stubbornly even in the face of his desires.

Allatu's laugh was empty. "Of course, you shall keep the farm, Samir. Whatever it is worth. Nevertheless, we should begin packing." With her final command, she turned expectantly and clapped her hands. "I will let Reshma handle the affairs of packing what you will need to bring. Mind you—" she turned to the woman who was glaring at her "—I do not want any of these things—" she gestured to the cheap knickknacks on the shelves "—in the new home. I shall handle making it look extraordinary. You should only pack what essentials you and the children will need. Samir, you will send Aadil into town when he returns with my wine and deliver a list to a few shops for items we will need. My Mistress," she turned to Luja. "You and I will speak privately, please." She did not wait for anyone to argue or question whether they would follow her orders. She stepped outside into the sunlight, leaving everyone in a silent storm behind her.

Chapter Four

Aadil enjoyed his trips to and from town as the family prepared for the move to their new home. Allatu was mysterious as to the location of their destination and refused to give details, except only that they would all be pleasantly surprised.

Luja had not felt this vibrant in years. She happily packed her scarves, her toiletries, and a few items of clothing she felt she would need for travel. Hala skipped through the house as well, singing songs and delighting Allatu with her sharp tongue and quick wit. The two older girls followed their mother's lead and avoided Allatu at all costs. Samir spent his time staring at Allatu's breasts when he thought no one was looking.

"The lady Allatu says we are to leave in the morning. I'm excited for the trip, Grandmother. I want to see our new house. Do you think it will be a really big house? Do you think Allatu is human? Mother doesn't like her at all—"

"Hush child. You speak too loudly. We do not want to upset Allatu, do we?"

"I don't think she cares much," Hala said as she spread out on her grandmother's bed and lifted her feet in the air, swinging them back and forth as if she was running.

"Stop that. What would you do if your father walked in? He would tell you that you are being indecent. I can see your underthings," Luja snapped. Despite her enjoyment of the strange creature they hosted, she worried about the effect on her youngest and most wild granddaughter.

Hala rolled over onto her stomach, resting her head in her hands. "Grandmother, Allatu says I should not hide myself under all of these clothes. She says I could grow up like a princess and that I can do whatever I wish."

Luja turned to face Hala with a serious expression. "Child, I know you enjoy our guest as I do, but she comes from a different time. She does not understand our ways and the place a woman holds in a home. You will marry a proper man and conduct yourself in a proper manner."

"What time does she come from? How old is she?"

"I do not know and I dare not ask."

"You may ask of me whatever you wish, my Mistress." Allatu appeared in the doorway, draped in a stunning blue dress embellished with gold coins that made tinkling noise with her every step.

"I apologize, Allatu, dear. She is young and curious."

"Of course, she is. And fearless, too, no doubt. You wish to know how old I am, little one? I lost count, truth be told." Allatu sat on Luja's bed and stretched her legs out like a cat, tilting her head as she inspected her satin slippers. "I was born here, did you know?" Both Luja and Hala shook their heads. "It was many, many years ago. Let me see… it was a time when we worshiped the Gods. We have many Gods, you know. I lived in a time when we had to fetch water from the rivers in order to wash our clothes and cook. Egypt ruled then… "

"Egypt? You mean… that long ago?"

"Yes. There were many Egyptians that came to Tunisia as merchants and traders. Others were not as welcome… " A dark look crossed Allatu's face. The frown did not diminish her beauty, it simply made her look even more appealing.

In an effort to fill the silence, Luja went back to arranging her scarves as she spoke. "I am certain you have seen many truly amazing things. I can only imagine what that might be like."

"I think it's exciting! I should want to live forever, too, like you, Allatu." Hala bolted up and smiled. "I would become a powerful woman and make fighting wars against the law. And killing wouldn't be allowed, either. Only really bad men would be killed. Oh… and everyone would have to be nice to animals. That would be the most important law."

Allatu's dark look disappeared and she laughed, brightening the room once more. "You would make a wonderful ruler! I do think I like you, little Hala. You remind me of myself when I was young. I was precocious, too." She whispered the last bit to Hala, who giggled.

"May I ask, Allatu, where are we going tomorrow? Will you not tell me?" Luja asked, a bit hesitant.

"Of course, I will tell you, Mistress, if that is your wish. It is to a place I lived many years ago by the sea. It is my favorite home. It is large, floors made of mahogany and high ceilings painted with the most beautiful murals. The tiled gardens that overlook the ocean are a favorite of mine. You will see, tomorrow."

"How will we get this house? I do not understand how such a thing can happen overnight," Luja said as politely as she could.

"How is anything done in this world? One seed falls to the earth and is buried under the dirt. Between the rains and the sun, it grows and becomes beautiful until it dies and the cycle is repeated again. So it is with all things, one thing ends to begin another." Allatu stood and smiled. "I shall be gone this evening. I will return before the morning comes. There are things I must tend to as well."

"See you tomorrow, Allatu," Hala said with a bright smile.

Allatu curtsied low with a graceful flourish. "'Til tomorrow, my future ruler of the land." Hala laughed and Allatu swept from the room. Luja tuned out the chattering from Hala as she thought of Allatu's explanation. She did not fully understand what she meant by flowers dying and growing again. She knew her grandmother would have understood it though. It made her heart ache still thinking of her. Luja fought a deep sense of foreboding as she sent Hala to play outside so she could continue packing. She told herself it was only the move that had her nervous. She adamantly hoped that was the truth.

***

Her Mistress and family were settling in for the night as Allatu stepped out into the dying light and waited for the sun to fall. She breathed deep and wiggled her toes in the dirt. The family garden was badly overgrown and needed more than a little attention. Slowly, Allatu walked around, poking into potted plants and explored the many gardening tools that collected rust and spider webs.

It was in the furthest corner of the garden she heard a noise. Surveying the yard, she knew no one was there. The noise was hollow, a deep drumming sound that vibrated inside of her, willing her to come closer. She stepped nearer to an unkempt olive tree and saw where the earth was recently upturned. Bending down, she ran her hands just above the mound of dirt and felt the force of the magic that lay beneath.

"This is where it lies. It is here." She placed her hand on the dirt and felt the *THUMP THUMP THUMP* from the statue below. She hesitated a moment and then whispered, "Rest well." She turned and walked out of the garden and into the night.

***

The sun crept over the horizon as Allatu made her way back to the home of her Mistress. She looked forward to leaving this place. It was quaint, yes, but she desired a more lavish setting surrounded by beauty. As she entered the garden to let herself in the back door, her Mistress stood in the garden sipping a cup of tea.

"Is everything prepared, my Mistress?" she called out.

With a start, Luja turned, spilling some of her tea as she did. Her eyes grew wide when she saw Allatu. "My dear, what is that all over your hands? Is that blood?"

The strange creature laughed, tossing her head back. "Of course, it is blood, my Mistress. I am the Servant of the Blood after all."

"Whose blood is it?" Luja felt the foreboding wrestle inside her, joined by a small seedling of regret.

"Whose blood?" Allatu looked down at her hands as if seeing it for the first time. "I do not know his name. His name matters not to me. He served a purpose, that is all."

"You killed someone, Allatu?" The beautiful creature smiled, reminding Luja of a wild tiger she saw once in a zoo. She remembered thinking of how beautiful and sleek the tiger was until she saw the size of its claws and realized how deadly was.

"My magic requires blood, Mistress. If you want these things for your family, then others must pay the price." She turned to go and spoke over her shoulder as she did. "We should leave as soon as possible. It will be a long trip and I am anxious to leave."

Luja nodded without an answer but she knew Allatu did not notice. She knew she should be sorry about whatever poor soul Allatu killed, but she rationalized that, since she did not know him, it could not possibly affect her. Therefore, she fought back the foreboding and regret once more in order to focus on the only positive ahead. They were leaving for a better life. Whatever price was paid for that, she accepted with a heavy heart.

Chapter Five

They travelled for most of the morning in the family car, headed toward the coast. Allatu did not care for it at all and complained the whole way joined by Hala. Aadil and the girls seemed fearful, but remained silent. Reshma's silence was deafening. She glared and refused to answer anyone who spoke to her. She resented the newcomer. She resented her mother-in-law for bringing her there. She even seemed to resent Hala for liking Allatu as much as she did. However, she reserved her most heated glares for her husband who seemed completely undeterred despite her nasty disposition.

Allatu pointed in the direction Samir was to drive and soon they found themselves approaching a large gated driveway.

"Father, where are we?" Aadil asked, sitting up, straining to see beyond the enormous iron gates.

"We should turn back now," Reshma said, but quickly bit her tongue after seeing the look on her husband's face.

"We have arrived." Allatu proclaimed. She then stepped out of the car and stretched like a gloriously dark and terrifying cat. Hala jumped out, ever on her new idol's heels and tried to copy her graceful stretch. Luja laughed a little at the sight of the child trying so hard to measure up to a woman who was nothing less than a goddess.

"What are we to do now? You said this would be my home and here I am waiting at this gate like a common beggar. If you lied to me—"

"My Lady. I am pleased you have arrived." A man's raspy voice cut Samir off. Everyone turned to look at the man who spoke from the other side of the gate. He wore clothes that went out of fashion many years ago, loose fitting and embroidered with silk thread. Luja had not seen clothes like his since she was a child and read about the ancient people of North Africa. His face was covered, leaving his eyes the only part of him visible. With a gloved hand, he opened the gate and bowed low as Allatu passed him.

"Come meet us at the house." She turned followed by the mysterious man and walked up the driveway.

"I want to go with Allatu," Hala cried.

"Get in the car, girl." Samir growled. She did, but not without a bit of fuss. Luja was sure she would have paid for her attitude in a painful way, were Samir not as excited as he was. With a leer that made Luja's skin crawl, Samir drove slowly up the driveway.

"Mother, look!" Jammana cried out then promptly covered her mouth with her hand. Everyone was staring at the elaborate mansion that sat on the side of a cliff.

"Is this true? Can this be mine?" Samir said to himself. Luja fought the urge to tell him no, that it was hers, but she stayed silent. Hala would not sit still as the car came to a rolling stop before an atrociously large mansion with two enormous white doors. Allatu stood at the top with the mysterious covered man directly behind her.

"Let us get out of this car. I need to stretch my legs." Luja said and she was out of the car, followed by Hala before anyone else dared to move.

"Come on," Hala cried out then she bounded up the steps to bounce up and down in excitement beside Allatu. In moments, curiosity got the better of everyone and they piled from the car, staring up at the house that was to be theirs.

"Well, let's get on with it," Luja prompted and they took the first tentative steps together.

The shrouded man opened the large double doors and welcomed them in with a bow.

Luja felt her son roughly brush past her in an effort to be the first one to enter the house. Any other time, she would have felt terribly put out by such a rude act from her son but as she entered the home—their new home—she was too breathless to care.

The floors were newly polished mahogany, as Allatu had said. The grand foyer boasted a Persian rub of deep crimson and gold. Luja took care not to step on the rug for fear of getting it dirty. Samir, however, stood with his hands on his hips and surveyed his new kingdom.

"How is this mine? Tell me this is no joke you are playing on me, woman," he demanded. A heavy silence fell over the group. The girls averted their eyes, staring blankly at the floor. Luja watched Allatu for a moment, but was even more transfixed by the venomous look in the mysterious man's eyes. She would have to watch out for that one.

Allatu approached Samir with a predatory look. "They say a wealthy Roman General took over this home and made it grand," she laced her arm through his and smiled. "The previous owner fell ill suddenly and now the home is yours." She pulled slightly on his arms and he followed her breaking away from the sight of her breasts only to stare open-mouthed at the gold inlayed staircase. "Beneath these carpets is all the original marble. Truly a wonder."

She continued to chatter on about the history of each statue or the artist who painted the murals on the ceilings. She pulled Samir further and further away, leaving Luja and her family with the mysterious covered man.

"How many bedrooms are there?" Aadil asked, taking a tentative step onto the stairs. Everyone turned to look at the mysterious covered man for an answer.

"There are nine suites available. The first and most grand belong to the Lady Allatu. I will alert the help and they will show you to your rooms." The man's voice was very deep. Luja did not have time to study him further because he turned abruptly and left them all alone in the grand foyer.

"It is like a castle, Mother. We're all grand royals, now," Hala called out from the stairs. "Come, Aadil, let's go explore."

"No!" Reshma snapped. "Not alone. We do not know who else is here." She looked up as she spoke at the expansive ceilings that were more ornate than anything she had seen before.

"Madam." The mysterious man returned with two small children, covered from head to toe as he was. "These are my children. They will be of service to you." The smallest, possibly close to Hala's age, stepped forward and bowed. The other was slightly older and stepped forward with a bow as well. Luja could not tell if they were boys or girls. They kept their heads bowed and were as silent as death. The mysterious man motioned for the children to go and they hurried up the stairs. Hala and Aadil hurried to catch up with them.

"Go with them, girls." Luja said. Both girls glanced at their mother for approval. She nodded, still inspecting her surroundings with a frown. Both older girls hurried up the stairs after their younger siblings.

"My son is unloading your belongings from the car. If you would follow me, I will escort you both to your rooms." Luja followed immediately. Reshma hesitated a moment, looking back over her shoulder, presumably for her husband, before continuing up the stairs.

The man took them up the long wide stairs and bade them to follow him to the right. Luja walked slowly, taking in the elaborate paintings that she was sure were painted by someone famous but she was not cultured enough to know who. The lavish carpets muffled their footsteps as they rounded a long hallway. They could hear the chattering of the children as the man lead them further.

He stopped at a door and opened it. "Your rooms, Grandmother." He extended his hand welcoming her inside and she stepped into a lovely sitting room. "Your bedroom is through the door there." He pointed to the door to the right. "Your washroom is there, Madam." He turned to Reshma. "Your rooms are just across the hall. If you would follow me." He did not wait for her to respond and left Luja's rooms.

Once alone, Luja took a deep breath and sank into a soft couch made of silk. "What have I done?" she whispered.

"Grandmother! Come look at my room! Oh…your rooms are beautiful, too. My bed is twice as large as my old one. Come see, Grandmother. Come see." Luja laughed a little. Hala's excitement was catching.

"Very well, child. You lead the way." Luja pulled herself up with a little difficulty and followed Hala as fast as she could. When she reached Hala's door, she saw Reshma and the older girls talking excitedly amongst themselves.

"Grandmother, have you seen our rooms?" Daayna exclaimed with uncharacteristic enthusiasm.

"I have come to do just that. If they are anything like my rooms, I shall be impressed indeed." And she was. Each child's room was decadent, to say the least. The plush rugs fit perfectly in each room. Daayna's room was a soft lavender with off-white trim. Fresh flowers sat on every tabletop and her bedroom overlooked an expansive garden below. Jammana's room was a bit warmer, decorated in peacock green and blue. The plush pillows and gold sconces made Luja feel as if she were in Marrakesh. Aadil's suite looked as if it belonged to a king. Deep purples and maroon silk wall coverings suited his serious nature perfectly.

"Come see mine now!" Hala said, half dragging her grandmother across the hall. Luja stepped into Hala's sitting room and found herself in the most ostentatiously decorated room yet. The room was circular with a large circle rug in the center. The walls were bronze with delicate pink flowers painted at the borders. A large crystal chandelier hung from the middle of the room. On the farthest part of the room sat her canopied bed with gold drapes and a soft pink coverlet.

"Isn't it the most beautiful thing you've ever seen, Grandmother?" Hala said.

"It certainly is. Where is your father?" Luja turned to the girls in Hala's doorway and they all looked at their mother. Reshma's expression went from light to dark in a moment. "I shall go find him." Luja started from the room and, as she rounded the hallway, almost ran into a young man carrying their bags.

She was startled and made her apologies only to be met with silence. The young man was covered as his father was, for this had to be the son of the mysterious man. Their eyes were quite alike. As she passed him, she caught a strange smell and decided to speak to Allatu about the boy washing a bit better in the future.

***

It took Luja almost an hour to make her way through the house before she found Allatu and Samir in the main drawing room whispering to one another.

"My son," Luja said. Both looked up, one with a guilty expression and the other with a dazzling smile.

"My Mistress. How do you find your accommodations? Is everyone happy with their rooms?" Allatu stood and stalked across the room. The table was set with a vat of wine in a crystal decanter. She poured red wine into one cup but looked up, questioning the other two if they wanted one as well. Both Samir and Luja shook their heads. "It is a good year. Although, I have had better. Samir," she said with a seductive smile as she lightly brushed his thigh. "Tell your mother what we have decided about the party."

"It will be here, of course," Samir said with an air of importance. "We will start sending out invitations to all of the important people soon. Allatu assures me she will handle the details."

"Indeed, I will. As is my duty. I shall need a few things, however..." Her voice trailed off as she took another sip of wine.

"Yes, yes. Whatever you need to do. I want this to be perfect. I want all of the wealthiest families here. No children, though. I will not have a gaggle of rug rats stomping around my new home." He pointed to Allatu and she nodded.

"Of course."

"Allatu, dear, I wonder if I might inquire as to the… the help you have hired? What are their names and where did you find them?" Luja watched Allatu's face, but saw no change in her expression.

"Oh, them. They are a family I found that needed a change in their status. I took the liberty of giving them the servant's quarters upstairs in the attic. The children are mute, as is the old woman. The father is the only one who will speak. If you need anything from them, just ring the little bell on your bedside table. They will scurry right over to tend to your every need."

"Why can't they speak?" Luja asked. It was such a strange thing that only one person in an entire family would be able to speak. Perhaps they were deaf as well? But that couldn't be so or they would not hear the servant's bell.

Allatu shrugged. "That is their way. I do not question it. They needed to be free of their past situation and I gave them the aid they looked for. I did them quite the favor, Mistress."

"I see. Very well." Luja still was not certain how she felt about the explanation but saw she would get no further now. She decided to speak to the father as soon as she was able.

"Good, let us get back to planning. I want everything perfect. I also want new clothes," Samir demanded.

"Yes, of course. For your family as well, I presume?" Allatu asked in between sips of wine.

Samir waved his hand impatiently. "Yes, yes. But my clothing should be the most expensive and of the best quality. I cannot walk among my guests in my new home in rags," he said a bit peevishly.

"Of course, you should not. I shall see to that immediately. As well as the rest of the family. In the meantime, we should step out onto the back balcony. The pool is so lovely!" Allatu opened the double glass doors from the parlor and Samir followed. Luja stepped out slowly, feeling the wave of doom overtake her again.

However, the view when she went outside swept all of the negative feelings away. The sun was bright in the sky and all she could see was the blue ocean surrounding them. The mansion sat quite high on a cliffside so they overlooked a dock far to the right and the neverending coast on the other. Allatu took them to the furthest side of the balcony that turned into a network of white archways. Inside of these sat the largest swimming pool Luja had ever seen. The bottom tiles were blues and green and they made the color of the water seem even more surreal.

Fountains bubbled happily, surrounded by colorful plants that bloomed in a variety of colors. The smell was her favorite part. The salty sea air filled her lungs. The happiness and relief of their good fortune made her heart glad.

She turned to go back inside and saw the children led by the two mute servants and followed by Reshma, headed to the pool.

She smiled at their squeals of delight and watched as the young girls seemed to blossom before her eyes and even serious little Aadil smiled up at his father. Her family was happy. They had all they could ever want and then some. Whatever price she must pay for this, she would willingly do it again. Resigned to try her luxurious bed, Luja excused herself to take a nap and let go of any regrets she might have.

Chapter Six

The party was scheduled for the following evening. For the past two weeks, the mansion hummed with people coming and going. Food for the party arrived in large trucks. Decorations arrived and were expertly placed by the professionals Allatu hired. The mute servants were the ghosts of the mansion. Over the weeks, any time either of them came near Luja, her skin crawled. However, with the beehive of activity, she was never able to speak with the man in private. She was curious about him and his silent family.

The children spent their days in the luxurious swimming pool, squealing and splashing one another. Aadil would run and drop into the pool making a large splash that delighted the girls. Reshma found her place in the home when the gaggle of tailors arrived. For days, they sewed and stitched one of a kind outfits for the girls. A whole other group was working on clothes for Samir and Aadil. Reshma oversaw all of it and Luja was happy for that. Her daughter-in-law seemed much more at ease and even slightly amiable at times.

The meals were prepared and served promptly at appointed mealtimes. Allatu waved away Luja when she attempted to be of help in the kitchens. "It is not proper for my Mistress to tarry away in the hot kitchen. I shall find you suitable duties as your status permits." That is how Luja found herself overseer of the seating chart for the formal dinner.

Many of the names on the list in her hands were unknown to her. A few she had only heard of in passing or on the news. A few were actual celebrities and politicians. The few she did know were merchants and businessmen from their hometown. Most, if not all, Samir owed money to in the past. Now, with his grand coming out in high society, he wished for them to see him in all of his glory. Her son, so desperate for people to recognize his greatness, wanted the night to be lavish and over the top.

Luja sat with a large poster on the table before her and little scraps of paper with the guest's names on them. She arranged them as she was instructed by Allatu. The most important were closer to Samir and his family. The least important, those who knew him in his previous situation, would be farther away. As he put it, they were to adore him from afar but they were not good enough any longer to sit with him.

Having run out of tea and stuck on where to put a Mister Farooqi, whom she was told was a very large man and needed extra room, Luja decided to take a walk to clear her mind. Her back no longer hurt, for that, she was quite thankful. Her bed cradled her as if she slept on a cloud.

Feeling quite relaxed and, for the first time since they moved, a little more at home. Luja leisurely made her way through the parlor and into the back hallways where many of the party preparations were commencing. Wooden beams and rolls of fabric stood in rows down the hallway. Luja felt the soft cloth as she passed them, relishing the feel of them between her fingers.

She was so lost in the beauty of the decorations, she did not realize she was not alone any longer. She heard a hushed conversation around the corner. Without hesitation, Luja crept closer to the end of the hallway and took refuge between two large bolts of white satin. Straining, she heard pieces of the conversation that was, apparently, between two people.

"There is nothing I can do—"

"Must… get… free… no… stay… "

"I will try. I do not know how. Do as she says and stay quiet."

"Hate... her."

"I know, Momma." She heard a rustle of clothes. "And you must hide this always."

After a few moments, Luja could not hear anything more, so she stepped carefully from her hiding place. Careful not to bring any notice to herself, she turned and made her way back from where she came. As she made her way up the stairs to her rooms, she went over everything she overheard. Who was the mysterious man speaking with? His mother, he called her. That would mean that was the old woman in the kitchens. Allatu said she could not speak. If that were true, which it apparently wasn't, why did she hear the old woman speak? Why would Allatu lie to her?

"My Mistress, is something troubling you?" Luja jumped.

"No, Allatu dear." She tried to calm the hammering in her chest at the sight of the ethereal woman. She stood in the doorway with her hands folded in front of her in such a way as to look nonthreatening. She wore an elegant dress of crimson and white that was a stark contrast to her dark skin. "Well, to be perfectly frank, my dear, I am a little troubled."

"Troubled? What can I do, Mistress? Tell me what is troubling you and I will see it gone." She approached her mistress and placed her hand on the elder woman's shoulder.

"It is the servants that have me troubled, truth be told. I heard the man speaking to his mother, the woman in the kitchens, earlier. I was under the impression she and the others did not or could not speak. But she did. What she said was quite alarming."

"What did the wench say?" Her calming demeanor changed as well as her tone. Underneath all of her beauty raged a beast Luja did not want to unleash, even on an unknown woman in the kitchen. Images of Allatu's hands covered in blood flashed in front of her eyes and she swallowed.

"She… she well, she tried to speak, you see. Said something about the kitchens being too hot. Are we caring enough for the help, dear? Should we not make sure they are more comfortable?" Luja's heart was racing. She did not know why she lied exactly, only she was afraid of what Allatu would do to the woman if she knew the truth. All of a sudden, it was quite clear who the old woman hated so much and who the man feared.

"Oh, is that all?" She laughed and wrapped her arm around Luja's shoulders, her smile and relaxed expression returning. "You are a kind mistress. I shall see to it immediately and let them know it was you who wanted them to be more comfortable. We are so lucky to serve you, my sweet Mistress."

Luja smiled and patted Allatu's hand. On the inside, she felt the repressed doom and guilt bubble up and explode. This woman was dangerous. Far more dangerous than she could have ever imagined.

***

Luja did not sleep well that night. Besides the hammering and constant flow of people working on the decorations until all hours, she could think of nothing except her own grandmother.

Her memory was good, but she had to close her eyes and concentrate to bring the image of her beloved grandmother to her mind. She remembered her hair was almost all white and her fingers bent in odd angles due to arthritis. She refused modern medicine, saying it was poison. Instead, she treated her ailments with poultices, teas and warm compresses at night.

She knew things, Luja's grandmother. She knew all about the moon's cycles and a host of other things Luja wished she would have paid attention to. Now, she could scarcely conjure her face. She would have wept if not for the fear in her heart for her family. Her grandmother, who knew so much, told her she would never dare to call upon the Servant of the Blood. Luja, forever impulsive and naive, should have listened. She could not ask her grandmother for help now. In fact, there was no one left to ask for any information. She was the last of her mother's side. She and Hala were the last two who knew anything of the statue and the family curse. "Well, I suppose it's up to me then," she said to the empty room.

Luja spent the rest of the evening sitting beside the window, staring out at the reflection of the moon on the dark ocean. There was little that she could do to change what had already happened, she knew that. But she could change the way things went from this point forward. After the party, she would sit Allatu down and set new terms. She had given Samir free reign to ask for whatever he wanted. In doing so, Allatu was becoming more and more dangerous. Whomever she killed before they left the farmhouse and whomever these servants were that hated her so would be the last of the guilt Luja would be responsible for.

***

The morning of the party dawned early to incredible smells coming from the kitchen and noise coming from everywhere. The children ran about, making nuisances of themselves while their mute servants watched over them. The older girls giggled and gossiped about their new dresses they would wear. Even Reshma seemed excited as she pointed the caterers to the kitchens and flower deliveries to the outer courtyard.

Samir made himself comfortable at the head of the overly large dining table while he ate an elaborate breakfast and read the paper. Luja joined him and was immediately served tea by the mysterious man.

"Your breakfast will be out in a moment, Madame," he rasped.

"Thank you—"

"Mother, you do not need to thank a servant. It is their job. Go." He waved the man away. "Now Mother, tonight must go perfectly. I looked over the seating chart for the dinner and I think you did fairly well. I made a few changes here and there but now it is perfect." He patted her hand and gave her an empty smile.

Luja tried to hide her displeasure at having all of her thoughtful work redone as soon as she stepped away from it. What did she care, really? Who sat where was hardly the most pressing issue now. A beautiful woman with a clipboard in her hand drew Samir's attention away from the newspaper. She was exotic and darker than any woman Luja had ever seen. When she smiled, she was certain she heard Samir whimper. She needed signatures on delivery papers, but Samir jumped out of his seat and ushered her to his study. Luja snorted into her cup of tea. Samir with a study. Ludicrous. He had never studied anything in his life.

"Your breakfast, Madame. Will there be anything else? I must see to many things this morning."

"Yes, of course, thank you. If I need anything, I shall get it myself." The man nodded and turned to go but Luja called out to him. "Wait! One thing I would like to know. What is your name? I was never told your name." The man turned slowly and stood rigid with his hands folded in front of him.

"My name w-is Zaabit, Madame."

"It is nice to finally meet you properly, Zaabit. And your children? What are their names?" Zaabit looked terribly uncomfortable now and she thought his coloring was paler than normal. "Perhaps another time, then. I'm sure you are too busy to stand there chatting with an old woman." Zaabit bowed slightly and left the room without another word.

Any other time she would have thought his departure extremely rude. Given this situation, it seemed perfectly natural for the man to fear her. With a start that made her hand tremble, she realized that *she* was the master of the monster that they feared. She placed her teacup down and patted her lips with a napkin.

"Right. I'll get to the bottom of this myself." She stood and headed through the servant's door that would take her to the kitchens.

The hallways were wide but darker than the rest of the house. It was also the only portion of the house that was not painted pure white or boasted plush carpeting. It was easy to find her way into the big kitchen due to the amount of noise there was. She opened the door and felt a blast of hot air from the many fires and boiling pots. Some of the most delicious smells she had ever inhaled filled her nose and made her stomach rumble with delight.

She was also surprised at the number of people working in there. She had been under the impression the old woman, Zaabit's mother, was the only one who worked in the kitchen. Looking around, she counted seven people buzzing about. They were all women with the exception of one other man who sat on a stool stirring a ridiculously large pot. She heard strange sounds coming from the direction of the women and turned back to them. They were hurriedly covering themselves as they had apparently taken off the garb they wore in the heat of the kitchen.

"I am sorry, dears. I didn't mean to startle you. I was looking for Zaabit's mother." Luja's question was met with expected silence. "Just a word is all I need." Luja tried to make her voice as soft and soothing as she possibly could. Every single one of the kitchen servants had their heads down except the one, slightly hunched figure at the end.

The hunched figure took a few tentative steps forward and opened her palms upward in supplication.

"I wonder if we might speak... uh... in private, if you please." Luja said with a smile. The old woman nodded and extended her arm for Luja to come with her.

Luja heard the other servants go back to work as she followed the old woman to a large pantry filled with food. The woman stopped and folded her hands behind her back with her head bowed.

"Thank you. I know you have many things to do today but I wanted to ask you if you could tell me your name." This made the old woman stiffen, then shake her head no. "I must confess to you, I know you can speak. I accidently overheard you and your son, Zaabit. I do apologize dear, and don't want to put you on the spot only... I wondered if there was anything you could... well, it's Allatu." She lowered her voice barely above a whisper. "I did not know what she was. I still do not." The woman's shoulders moved as she breathed deeply in silence. "Please. I need to know more about her. I fear for my family—" The woman slammed her hands down on a stack of crates causing Luja to jump. After a few moments, she pulled herself together and pointed to the door. Luja knew it was futile to question her further. "I am sorry to have bothered you," Luja said before leaving the old woman shaken and trembling in the pantry.

***

The gown the tailors made for Luja was colorful and incredibly comfortable. It was red silk with silver tassels at the end. The shawl matched the dress, as did the red slippers she wore. Luja couldn't remember feeling so elegant. As she traced black charcoal around her eyes, she saw a glimpse of the young girl she once was.

"Foolish. That's what I was and even more so now," she said to her reflection as she turned to leave. The band was warming up downstairs as she descended the immense staircase. From behind, Hala called out to her.

"Grandmother! Wait for me." Little Hala looked every bit the princess in her indigo dress that sparkled with flecks of mirrors that caught the light in a brilliant display.

"My, don't you look wonderful, my little one," Luja said as Hala wrapped her arms around her grandmother's waist. "Let me look at you," She drew the girl away and made a spectacle of how grown up she looked. After a few moments of smiles and excited nods, the duo walked together to the front foyer where they would greet guests as a family.

Luja scanned the hustle of bodies for Allatu but she was nowhere in sight. The dark-skinned woman with the clipboard approached Luja and Hala motioning them to follow her. Apparently, the rest of the family was already in place.

"You stand here," she said, pulling Hala by the arm to stand at the end of the line of children. "And you are here, beside your daughter-in-law. There, that's good." Before Luja could utter a word, the beautiful woman was gone.

Many of the people hurrying to and fro were servants wearing the most elaborate costumes she had ever seen. Every color imaginable glittered under the soft candlelight up and down the main hall. When she turned toward the door, she finally saw her son, Samir, seated on an ornate chair as if he were Caesar himself. He wore a suit made of the purest white linen she had ever seen. Even the rose in his lapel was white. It was odd given the colorful surroundings, until she realized his was the only white in the mass of people.

"To better to see you with, my dear." Luja said under her breath. A tall, handsome man entered through the front doors and bowed low to Samir. They spoke in hushed tones before Samir nodded and the handsome man walked past the family toward the party staging area.

It was not long before streams of people began to arrive. Luja had never seen many of them before in her whole life. A few were famous faces she had seen in the papers. Politicians arrived with their security in tow. A few bewildered faces of former friends of Samir wandered in as if by accident. They were not dressed in near as fine of clothes as the rest of the guests. Samir smiled at them and greeted them with grace. She knew he loved this moment more than any other in his whole life. His acidic desire to best everyone at all costs was finally paying off. And this made Luja immensely nervous.

The woman with the clipboard approached them and spoke in a hurried, rushed tone. "Everyone is taking their seats. Dinner will be served as soon as you are in your places. Follow me, please." She said the last few words over her shoulder with the air of expectation that they would follow without question.

Samir walked ahead of the family, followed by Reshma, Aadil, the girls, and finally Luja herself. She was content to stay behind. In fact, she would have preferred to be left to watch the proceedings without being included in all of the fanfare. The girls were giggling together in excitement. Aadil walked behind his parents in an effort to appear far older than he was. Luja admired the artistry the decorators were able to accomplish on such short notice. They walked down the main hallway toward the back balcony where the guests were gathered around the pool.

Soft candles lit the main hallway that was draped with cloth in the Moroccan style. As they made their way to the archway nearest their seats, all eyes turned to watch them enter. The band began playing a lively tune and many people cheered. Samir smiled widely, waved, and shook hands with those he felt were most important. They took their seats at the lavish table of honor on actual gold chairs. Luja snorted, feeling preposterous as the servant behind her helped push her chair forward. Samir, however, remained standing. He raised his glass with a smile. The guests all stood and raised their glasses to him as well.

"My friends, I thank you all for taking the time out of your busy schedules to enjoy an excellent dinner with my family and me. We are truly blessed to have such wonderful friends." cheers erupted from the crowd and Samir's smile grew. "Enjoy the food and entertainment everyone." Applause and cheers continued as Samir took his seat. Reshma attempted a smile but it was forced and dry. The children beamed with happiness as a host of servants entered from behind swaths of cloth dancing in the breeze. Choreographed to perfection, they snaked their way between the dimly lit patios, serving the first course of the meal.

Luja scanned the crowd, noting Allatu's absence. Perhaps it was best, she thought, as one of the servants placed a delicate porcelain bowl filled with soup in front of her. Allatu would be a distraction and currently, Samir was enjoying the attention.

She lifted a small spoon with a deep bowl on the end and examined it. It was gold. Real gold. Once she looked closer, the handle was that of a serpent coiled around a woman's naked body. Feeling her cheeks flush, she glanced at Hala's

spoon and saw hers was a replica of the one Luja
had. All of her thoughts melted away as she tasted
the creamy cucumber soup. She closed her eyes and
relished the fresh, crisp taste. Before long, night fell
and everyone was chatting amongst themselves.
The music was low and mellow which added to the
euphoria of the night.

The next courses were beyond even Luja's
expectations. Candied plums dripped with caramel
sauce in a bed of wild rice. There was wild boar that
was cooked to perfection and tasted heavenly. It
was not a particularly fatty beast so Luja was able to
enjoy the taste. An emu was brought out, cooked
whole, carried by four servants on a portable dais.
The crowd ooh'd and ahhh'd as two servants began
to carve the massive beast. The other two pulled out
long sticks and lit the ends on fire. They danced
about the tables, dramatically blowing fire into the
night, as the other two carved slices of the animal
and placed them on silver plates carried by the
servers.

Luja found she was quite enjoying herself.
She looked around to see her family smiling, joyful,
and well fed. Perhaps she had been wrong to
question her decision about Allatu. Perhaps it was
the wine, but she felt more relaxed than she had in

days. She even joined in on the applause as the fire breathers bowed and extinguished their flames.

She helped herself to seconds of the roasted lamb in mint sauce. She had always loved the flavor but this one tasted particularly delicious. Hala and Aadil earned a stern look from their mother after having a battle with peas and boiled onions.

The cool night breeze mingled the smells from the food and the ocean together into an intoxicating mixture. Before long, the children were yawning, and quickly, the servants came to fetch them away. For some unknown reason, Luja looked around and saw the two mute children of Zaabit standing in the shadows waiting to tend to their charges. Her unease returned in full force when Zaabit himself appeared and stood behind the children, a hand on either of their shoulders.

A change in the energy of the room brought Luja's attention back to her plate. Servants entered through cloth covered archways to bring out the final dish of the evening. In groups of five, the servants carried towers of desserts to each of the tables. Raspberries and chocolate truffles dripping with a sweet sauce glittered on her plate. As she took a tentative bite, she watched the euphoric atmosphere of the guests. No one was happier than

Samir, however. Every few minutes, a new guest approached him with reverence and whispered to him with smiles and friendly shakes of the hands. They laughed. They patted one another on the back. Samir was finally where he wanted to be. Luja had to admit she was happy with where they were as well and resolved to reign in Allatu's wish fulfillment the next day.

Reshma was not accustomed to drinking and was quickly falling asleep at the table. With a disgusted look from Samir, he waved to one of the passing servants and had them escort her to her rooms. Once she was gone, Samir's spirits lifted and a wicked smile crossed his face. He stood and everyone immediately fell silent.

"I hope you have enjoyed this marvelous feast tonight." Cheers and calls of *"Bravo"* echoed in the night. He smiled and raised his hands for silence. "But the night is not over, my friends. There is entertainment as well." Whoops and applause filled the night that made even Luja laugh. "Indeed. In honor of tradition, tonight we will host two separate entertainment events. The lovely ladies in attendance tonight will find their amusement there!" with a flourish and gasps from the crowd, a troop of acrobats flipped and summersaulted from behind the main archway and bowed low. The fire breathers returned and stood on either side of the archways, blowing fire into the night. The acrobats spun through the room, stopping at each table to extend a hand of invitation to each woman. Luja was the last of the women to leave the tables but she did not go with them. Her curiosity got the better of her. Therefore, she settled herself in the shadows behind an extremely soft blue cloth that hung on the outline of the archway nearest the main table.

"Gentlemen," Samir said with a leer. "For us, the night's excitement has yet to begin." Rowdy cheers from the men exploded again as one very large man stood and made a scene by grabbing one of the servant girls. He laughed as the girl struggled to get away. "Careful now, don't want to peak too soon," Someone yelled and the men roared with laughter.

The servants exited and soon only the men remained. Luja could feel their excitement from both the promise of lurid delights and more alcohol. "I am a man of tradition," Samir continued. "I chose tonight's theatre especially for this occasion." From the opposite side of where Luja hid, curtains were pulled back by unseen hands. The men craned their necks as a multitude of women peaked out from behind it. They were so scantily clad, Luja was sure she saw breasts exposed and she wanted to look away. But she watched as the men stood as if under a spell. "Gentlemen, if you would, follow these lovely ladies." The women reached out from behind the shadows of the curtain beckoning them to come. All Luja could see as the men hurried toward the ladies were arms that glittered with jewels and even once a woman's backside.

In moments, the patio was empty. Samir followed the men down the hallway that would take them to the furthest portion of the back balcony. She knew there was a large silk tent elaborately decorated with pillows and candles in that direction. The tables were a mess and for once, Luja was delighted she would not be cleaning it all up.

"Madame," a hoarse voice rasped from behind her. Luja jumped, grasping her chest and turned to see Zaabit standing only a few feet away.

"Oh, dear… oh, dear. You frightened me," she stuttered as she tried to regain her composure. Zaabit put a single finger to where his mouth hid behind the veil that covered his face. Looking around once more, he motioned for her to follow him. Without a second thought, Luja nodded. Everyone was busy with festivities so there was little chance her absence would be noticed. She followed him down the empty hall that led to the kitchens. Instead of going through the door that took her to find his mother earlier, he made a sharp turn to the left and up another, more narrow, flight of stairs.

These stairs were without the plush carpets of the main part of the house. These much older stone stairs felt cold and hollow. Once they reached the top of the landing, she saw three doors in a row. He reached out and opened the nearest one. Zaabit stood to the side and waved Luja in. She was not sure what to expect but thought rightly that they were in the servant's quarters.

The room was sparsely decorated with two small beds and a shelf to put their belongings. A single candle burned on one of the nightstands, casting eerie shadows on the walls. The room smelled old and stale. Mixed with the staleness was another, more sweet and putrid aroma that she could not define.

"My family," Zaabit croaked. Sure enough, in the shadows there was his mother, his eldest son and the two small children who tended her own grandchildren.

"How do you do?" Luja attempted a smile but failed. The mute family stood together shrouded in darkness and their veils.

"You are the Mistress, yes?" Zaabit asked walking to his family's side. "You brought that creature here?"

"I… I am and I did. Although, I was ignorant to what that meant—"

"What it meant?" Zaabit broke in. "What it meant was our deaths." His words fell heavy on her heart.

"My dears, no one is going to kill you. Your life is not in danger." Luja pleaded with them. For the first time in a very long time, Luja began to feel afraid. Would they hurt her? Did they want to be released from their service to the house? She would gladly do so and wanted to tell them but Zaabit pushed his eldest son forward into the meager candlelight.

"No one will hurt us?" he rasped. He reached out and roughly pulled away the veil covering his son's face. He yanked until it and the front of the boy's shirt was open, exposing his chest. Luja felt the room spin as she backed slowly toward the door. "We are already dead, Mistress," he spit the last word out as if it were poison. "She did this for you." He pointed an accusing finger at Luja.

She could not move. She could barely breathe. The young man, no more than fifteen, stood with a gaping gash across his neck. His skin was the color of a stormy sky and all at once, Luja knew the pungent aroma in the room—Death.

"No. No. No," she whispered over and over as her hand tried to block the smell from invading her nose any further.

"You look at what you have done to my family. My children. My mother… all dead to serve you. She holds us here to serve your family. I cannot join my wife in death because of you." The words were hard for him to get out but Luja understood them all. She felt the man's pain. She did not want to see anymore but he was right, this was her fault.

"I'm so sorry… I did not know." Her eyes burned with unshed tears.

"You are sorry? Sorry? Look at my children! They were murdered in their beds so you and your family could have all of this," he waved his arms in the air. "I was her first victim," he raised his shirt and Luja felt bile rise in her throat. The hole in his chest was large. The skin peeled away as one would see a beast for slaughter. Black, rotting flesh outlined the hole in his chest. "She came to me first, before she killed my children. She has killed many more for you, Madame. Many more."

Luja covered her mouth and sank to the floor, shaking her head. The horror of the dead family standing before her made her ill. But the worst, the most painful part of it all, was that he was right. She did this to them. The old woman stepped forward and placed her hand on her son's arm. She mouthed a few unintelligible words to him and he nodded.

"My mother says you are a good woman. I want to know if she is right. You can send the creature back to the hell she came from. Once that is done, we will be able to die in peace. You are the only one who can help us."

"I don't know how, Zaabit. I barely knew what I was doing when I called her to us. I was desperate to help my family."

"As am I."

"Do you know how to send her back?" Luja asked looking at each of them in turn. They all shook their heads and Luja's hope fled.

"You can make her tell you. You have the power to make her tell you. You are her Mistress."

"Yes... yes. I will. I swear it." Luja made to stand but Zaabit stepped forward and helped her to her feet. "Thank you."

"You better return to the party. I will show you the way."

"There is no need," Luja said. "I know my way. I need a few moments to myself." She turned to leave the dark shadowy room but stopped at the door. "I am so sorry for what has happened to you. I will make it right. I swear it." The ghostly figures said nothing as Luja turned and left.

Chapter Seven

Luja's mind reeled as she made her way down the servant's stairs and back into the main area of the house. She heard music and laughter but her heart ached. The children... the poor children. Wiping tears on her scarf, Luja walked among the servants who were quickly clearing the tables of the feast. She stood in the middle of the patio and looked to her right. She knew the women were somewhere down the hall past the colorful swaths of cloth that led to the pool. To her left, Luja knew the men were there doing whatever it was that men did when their wives were not around.

For reasons she did not know, Luja decided to go to the left. She wanted to see what her son was doing. She also had a sinking feeling that there amongst the men she would find Allatu. She pushed the soft blue cloth to the side and entered the hall of arches that would take her to the silk tent she saw the day before. Before the party decorators, this was all an open area. One could see from this end of the patio all the way to the pool. The archways, built for support as well as beauty, now were draped with cloth that made it seem like a fairy tale. Every few feet, candelabras stood on small tables to light the way. She heard the drums pounding in a primal beat before she saw anything. She didn't want to enter the tent from the front, so Luja crept to the side where she knew the servants would be entering to refill drinks.

Dodging such a servant, Luja stepped behind a pillar and waited for them to pass. By happenstance, she found the perfect spot to hide from everyone but still watch what was going on inside. What she saw made her blush like a virgin on her wedding night.

The men were seated on large pillows around small tables. Everywhere Luja looked, women were draped over a man or one of the tables. One woman was completely nude and the men were using her as a table, eating little cakes from parts of her Luja would not want food to touch. Another woman danced, pulsating her hips in time with the music. She was nude but the most secret parts of her were covered in jewels. It was scandalous and beautiful. Luja found Samir with the dark-skinned woman who no longer held a clipboard. She was wearing a shockingly see-through dress and fed her son grapes with a smile. She watched him laugh at something the men around him said. She wanted his happiness and this is what Samir's happiness looked like. Disgusted, Luja wanted to turn away but she stayed. For some reason, she felt as though she needed to see. This night started hopeful and was quickly revealing her folly at every turn.

As if on cue, the music stopped and many of the dancing girls took their seats next to the men of their choice. A stillness filled the tent and Luja strained to see if anything was happening. Then softly the drums began again. Slowly, like a heart beating, the drummers commanded the silence of the guests with the sound. That was when Luja saw her. Allatu entered the tent as if she was sex personified.

Her costume was elaborately made. The skirt was layered in lavender and gold held together with an ornate belt made of large coins. Her breasts were covered, barely, with a purple top that matched the skirt. Her skin was painted in vibrant blue henna designs. Her fingers and wrists glittered in jewels. Nothing compared to seeing her this way. An elaborate headdress of gold framed her face. Ethereal and seductive, she moved to the center of the room and wantonly moved her hips. Every eye was fixated on the creature dancing. Many men, and a few women, held their breath as she danced closer to them.

Back and forth, her hips moved and her back arched in an almost inhuman way. Luja was not sure if Allatu danced to the beat of the drums or if it was the other way around. Allatu looked feral as she crawled across the floor. She was a wild thing. But only Luja knew she was far more dangerous than any of those watching her would ever know.

When the music ended, the tent erupted into a thunderous round of applause. The men regarded her with lustful glances as she stalked toward them. The women watched her, some with envy and others with awe, as she stood behind Samir and wrapped her arms around his neck, placing a lingering kiss on his cheek. He was the envy of many and he knew it all too well.

From out of the shadows, Luja saw someone who was familiar to her. It was the handsome man who had greeted Samir as the party guests arrived. He obviously knew Samir well because he approached his side full of assurance and ease. She noted many of the female's eyes watched him pass. However, it was the change in Allatu's expression that made Luja even more interested in the man.

Allatu watched him sit gracefully at Samir's side. What was astonishing was that the man did not look at Allatu once.

"Miracles do happen." Luja said to herself from her dark hiding place. Too interested in what more she might see in the tent of pleasure, Luja settled back and watched. The music started up again and a few of the scantily dancing girls convinced a few of the drunk, sweaty men to dance with them. They looked like baboons, thought Luja. But that's what drink did to people.

Samir was in deep conversation with the handsome man as Allatu stood over him as sentinel. Her beautiful doe eyes never left the remarkable man sitting beside Samir. He was not too tall and not too short, he was just right, Luja thought. The open-chested shirt he wore flattered his build. Luja could see the fine black hairs that trailed down his chest to the soft skin of his belly. If she were younger, she would have swooned. Now, with the wonderful memories of lying with a man behind her, she wished all of the adoring women luck. He was Persian, no doubt about that. Persian men, especially this one, had soulful eyes that could show both animalistic desire and formidable hatred. Luja knew a powerful man when she saw him. He tossed back a drink and laughed at Samir's joke. Still, noted Luja, not even glancing in the direction of Allatu.

Allatu, seemingly frustrated with his lack of attention, began a conversation with the man opposite of the host and the handsome man. She laughed. Loudly. She pouted her lips and batted her eyes and yet, the man seemed to ignore her presence. It was almost comical if Luja did not know already how deadly Allatu could be. She felt compelled to go over to the man and whisper a word of warning in his ear. She watched as Allatu stood and, after staring at the handsome man for a moment, turned and sauntered off into the shadows.

"Well, this is interesting indeed." Luja chuckled to herself. After finding out what sort of a monster she unleashed on the world, it was a nice respite to laugh a bit before dealing with the real issues at hand.

"My Mistress." Luja turned hearing Allatu address her. "I am sorry, my Lady. I did not mean to frighten you." She smiled but Luja caught a glimpse of a shadow in her eyes.

"My dear, I could not help but watch. The music was wonderful. And your dancing… makes one wish to go back in time."

"Is that what you would like, my lady? I could make you appear younger if that is your wish?"

"No. No, thank you." A spark of a plan began to come to life and Luja hoped she was doing right. "Although, I did notice that terribly dashing man beside my son. Who is he?" Luja pointed as if Allatu was unaware of the man.

"Oh." She came to stand very close to Luja and they both watched the handsome man drink and talk with others around him. "His name is Arman. He has come all the way from Egypt to come to this party. He wishes to remain here and be companion to your son. Is he not divine?" she said breathlessly.

"Oh, indeed, he is." Luja's mind was racing and she knew she very little time to act. "I see many of these ladies desire him. Why, look at that one there." She pointed to the topless girl with underthings made from gold chains. "She is practically begging him for attention. Looks like he fancies her." The truth was he merely glanced at the girl but no harm in piling it on when necessary.

"Does he? I cannot see why. She is a cow. I shall deal with her," Allatu snapped.

"You will do no such thing, Allatu." Luja said as calmly as she could. "Leave the girl be. I take it you would rather he fancy you instead?" she asked lightly although her heart was racing.

Allatu sighed heavily. Her frown was endearing. "I do not see why not. I should like a lover of my own. He suits me."

"Have you any reason to believe this man returns your affections?"

"No," Allatu's frown deepened. "I do not understand why."

"All this—" Luja waved her hand toward the mess of sweaty, drunk bodies roaming around. "—means nothing to a man like that. He does not want some trollop who dances about acting a fool. He wants a powerful woman and one who he considers his own." Allatu turned and listened intently. "You will never win a man like that, Allatu. I am sorry, my dear. But I do not think that man will take you as his own, under normal circumstances."

Allatu's eyes narrowed. "Normal circumstances?"

"Yes." She turned to regard the ethereal creature and had a moment of absolute clarity. Regardless of the magic that animated her and gave her power, she was once, and still was, a girl. "He is obviously from a family of means. You can see that in the way he carries himself."

"Yes, he is. However, he is the fourth brother and wishes to live here for a while. His father wishes for him to live on his own for a few years before inheriting his fortune."

"How is it you know so much about this man?"

Allatu looked abashed and folded her hands neatly in front of her. "I read a letter of introduction to Samir from his family here in Tunis. I was curious…" her voice trailed off and Luja smiled.

"So you want this man, do you?" Allatu nodded her head and adorably chewed on her bottom lip. It was the most human thing Luja had ever seen her do. "Then perhaps there is something we can do. Or rather, something I could do…"

"Mistress, do you mean you would wish this for me?" Allatu looked stunned.

"I could, my dear. For a price."

"Anything," Allatu declared without missing a beat.

"Indeed. Anything?" The girl nodded. "Very well. I will consider wishing for that man to give you what you want if you release Zaabit and his family from their unfortunate servitude."

"Release… Who is Zaabit?" The adorable frown returned to her face as she tilted her head to the side in confusion.

Feeling anger boil inside, Luja placed her hands on her hips and hissed, "The dead family living in my home. How dare you? It is an abomination and I will not have it. They will be released and buried properly. Immediately. You killed children, Allatu." The last words came out with effort and Allatu rolled her eyes in exasperation.

"Very well, Mistress. It was the best I could do under such short notice. I shall need to find new servants if I am to release them."

"Do it. And do it by morning."

"And what of Arman? Will you not wish this for me now?"

Luja turned from the girl and sighed. The night's events were weighing heavy on her but she could not rest now. Not yet. She needed to stay sharp. "Once Zaabit and his family are released and given a proper burial, we will discuss it."

"Yes, Mistress."

"Oh, my dear, one more thing," Luja turned and pointed a finger in the direction of her son. "Samir will no longer be making demands of you.

Any wishes fulfilled will go through me or not at all."

"Yes, Mistress." Allatu's voice was just shy of a whisper.

"Very well. I shall run along to see to the women. I doubt it is as exciting as all this, but I should make an appearance. In the morning, once we have all rested, let's you and I have a cup of tea to chat." Luja walked back through the covered hall toward the pool. Her legs shook and her heart was rattling in her chest but she felt good.

Chapter Eight

Luja found Zaabit lurking in the shadows on her way to the women's area. He stood as still as a statue, but when he saw her, he made a move as if to flee. He was covered once more from head to toe. But Luja remembered the sight of the black, acrid hole in his chest and shuddered.

Luja beckoned him to her, looking over her shoulder as she did to make certain they were not being watched. He stepped from the shadows and nodded in greeting.

She was vaguely aware that she was standing before a dead man but kept her visage as calm as possible. "Zaabit, I have spoken with Allatu. She will release you by morning, *Inshallah.* You and your family."

She heard a deep sigh come from him and he hung his head. "What of the others?" he whispered after a moment.

"Others?"

"Yes. The others in the kitchens... they, too should be released."

Feeling overwhelmed and a bit helpless, Luja ran her hand down her cheeks and sighed. "I have managed this much tonight. Tomorrow, I will address the others and their fates. Believe you me, I want this business over and done with as soon as possible."

"You will never be free of the darkness she brings unless you send her away. You must have her tell you how to do that. It is the only way."

"Yes. Yes, I understand. I need to see to the guests." Luja turned to go but stopped herself. She was acting horribly and she knew it. She turned back to the shrouded man and smiled sadly. "I am sorry, Zaabit. I am so terribly sorry for you and your family. May your souls rest easy and I shall beg your forgiveness with every breath I take. *Allah yerhamo.*"

Zaabit said nothing as she turned once again to leave. How was she to have known what calling Allatu would bring? *Oh, but you knew it was a risk,* Luja, she told herself. *Your own grandmother warned you. Now look what you have done.*

***

Once Luja reached the women's area beside the pool, she could hardly stand. Fatigue and an overwhelming sadness overtook her as she settled into a soft cushion chair and accepted a tall glass of fruit juice from one of the servants. This girl was all smiles so it was safe to say she was one of the living servants. That thought alone made her head pound. How had things come to this? When did she abandon her faith, her humanity, and her trust in her family?

She sipped her iced drink and watched the women chat with one another. Many were yawning. A few had even fallen asleep with their heads on the tables. Luja wondered if Zaabit and his family would celebrate or mourn the news she gave them. Would she pay for this in the afterlife? What would tomorrow bring? Would she have the courage to see her plan through? Too many questions and not enough sleep, she decided. Without finishing her drink, she excused herself from the party and made her way slowly up the massive stairs to her rooms.

***

Luja slept very little. Lying in her bed, she stared at the canopy and waited for the sun to rise.

Had Allatu released Zaabit yet? Was he now buried properly with his family? She whispered another prayer for his soul and asked again for forgiveness. Perhaps in time she would start to forgive herself.

Once night gave way to the murky gray morning, Luja pulled herself out of bed with a groan. Getting old was not fun nor was it pleasant. She set off for her morning ablutions, mindful that the rest of the house was still sleeping. The immense emptiness was heavy when she left her rooms in search of a morning cup of tea. Perhaps coffee this morning, she thought to herself as she slowly made her way down the stairs. The thought lifted her spirits slightly so she was in quite a pleasant mood by the time one of the mute kitchen servants came with a tray of bread and honey.

"Coffee please, dear, if you would." Luja saw the woman give a slight curtsy before dashing back behind the door that separated them.

"Good morning, Mistress." Allatu appeared in the doorway dressed in a flowing gown of white silk. The contrast to her brown skin was stunning. She could see her voluptuous breasts moving freely beneath the silk. Youth and beauty are indeed wasted on the young, she thought to herself with a sigh.

"Good morning, Allatu. Did everything go as planned this morning?" Luja asked, raising her eyebrows. The servant returned and froze a moment in the doorway when she saw Allatu standing there. Luja watched the girl place the tray of coffee on the table and set out her saucer. Luja's stomach turned. How reprehensible to have this poor woman wait on her while her killer was here watching, she told herself. "Thank you, I will pour. Off with you." She shooed the girl away, who was only more than happy to comply.

"You do not like the servants, Mistress?" Allatu asked absentmindedly, twirling a strand of her dark hair between her fingers.

"I rather prefer servants who are still living, Allatu. See to that in the future, would you?"

Allatu laughed merrily and then sighed. "It was a lovely party, was it not Mistress? Your family has risen to be the envy of all who know of you."

"Indeed. But you did not answer my question. What of Zaabit and his family?" She took a sip of coffee and felt the flavor fill her with pleasure.

"Yes, yes. All taken care of. They're in the ground just as you requested. Quite dead now." Allatu sat gracefully and lifted her hair from her neck, letting it cascade back down with a shake of her head.

"Good. Now, we have some things to discuss, you and I."

"Oh? What would have of me today? Shall I make you young and beautiful again?" she asked with a mischievous grin.

"No, thank you. I'm quite satisfied with one foot in the grave."

"Do not say things like that, Mistress." Allatu's expression was pained and suddenly serious.

"Why are you so worried, my dear? I only have one foot in it. The other is out and about." Luja chuckled at her joke while she blew into her cup of coffee.

"If something were to happen to you... I cannot allow anything to happen to you, Mistress. If you die, I go back into my sleep until called again." Allatu said softly.

Luja watched the creature sitting across from her at the table. She was so tremendously beautiful. It was almost scary how beautiful she was. Her eyes locked onto Luja's with a pleading look. There was much Luja did not know and the one who had all of the answers was sitting right across from her.

"Well, I'm not dead yet. So, don't fear." She took another sip of coffee and placed the cup softly on the table. She folded her hands and gave Allatu her full attention. "Now that we're here-"

"Madame, I am sorry to intrude." Arman entered apparently thinking the room would be empty this early in the morning. Luja's eyes flicked to Allatu then back to Arman.

"Not a problem, Arman. I'm happy to meet you, finally." He flashed a dazzling smile and approached her with ease.

"I wasn't aware we had been introduced. You must be Samir's mother, Luja," he extended his hand and she took it. He gently brought her wrinkled, arthritic hand to his lips and placed a kiss on her knuckles. Regardless of how old she was, she still felt the thrill of the man's touch.

"You have met Allatu, Arman?" Luja gestured to her companion who stood and attempted to look demure but failed utterly. She still oozed sex and Luja was quite certain, as the sun light filled the room, her white silk dress was see-through.

"I have." Arman gave Allatu a curt nod, then returned to Luja with a smile. "I came for coffee then I will take Samir out for the day. A few of his new friends require his company and I will drive him in my car. It should be a gas." His smile was infectious and Luja couldn't help but swoon a little over the dark eyelashes that framed his eyes and the small dimple in his cheek when he smiled.

"I am certain you two will be a hit. Before you go, Arman, could you see to it that no one disturbs us in here? Allatu and I have a bit of business to attend that I wish to get on with without interruption."

"Of course," Arman bowed low in an extravagant manner, bringing Luja's laughter bubbling out again. She shook her head as he left the room taking the glow with him.

"Why, Mistress, will he not tolerate even a glance in my direction? Am I not beautiful? Am I not desirable?" Allatu sat heavily into her chair once more with an adorable pout upon her face.

"Yes, you are all that and more. However, have you ever considered the fact that along with the beauty and the desire you are also quite terrifying?"

"Me? I am nothing of the sort."

"Are you not?" Luja asked again with a pointed look. "He is smart as a whip, that one. He knows you are more than just a pretty face."

"I suppose I am that. But still…" Her voice trailed off and Luja watched her, wondering what was going on in her mind.

"My dear, I have questions for you and I request you answer them fully and truthfully." Luja felt as if she blurted out her words but Allatu simply turned to her and nodded. "Good. Now, there are many things I do not know about… this…" she faltered not knowing the right word to use.

"You mean me. You do not know what I am. And this scares you?"

"Yes dear, to put it bluntly. I ask that you tell an old woman your story. I could tell you mine but I wager yours is far more impressive." Luja sat back with her coffee in hand and waited.

Allatu delicately brushed a strand of hair from her face then placed both hands on the table before her. "Where should I begin?"

"The beginning. When you were… not…. this."

"I see. Very well, Mistress. My name is and always has been Allatu. I was born not far from here. My family was poor. Incredibly poor. Until I was born, that is. From an early age, everyone could see how beautiful I was. As I grew older, men would come and beg my father for my hand in marriage." Allatu laughed. "These old, wrinkled men wanted to bed me even as a child. More even as I grew into womanhood. My father knew he would make a grand sum by marrying me to the wealthiest man he could find. Therefore, he waited and entertained every man who came from afar to see me.

"I remember my mother very little. She died of the plague when I was quite young. I had three brothers. They adored me, of course. They married and soon it was just my father and I. People whispered about Father, saying he was keeping me for himself but that was not the truth. Father would never hurt me. He wanted what was best for the family."

"Your family… you said, when you came, that you served the women of my family. Does that mean you and I are related?"

"No, Mistress. Your line is another matter. I will get to that."

"Yes, of course. Carry on." Luja sat back and watched Allatu recall her history with a dazzlingly adorable expression of concentration.

"It was when I was fully a woman. I believe it was my seventeenth year. I became aware of that a man from a neighboring tribe was desperate for my hand in marriage. I recall his name because of all of the men who loved me then, his was the love that took my life as I knew it."

"He caused this?"

"In a way. His mother was the one." A dark shadow crossed Allatu's face that made Luja close her mouth to any further questions. "He and his family traveled by camel in those days, Mistress," Allatu added for Luja's understanding. "They arrived with all of their belongings packed tightly in bundles. They did have a good amount of wealth for such a family. Goats, camels, and plenty of people to tend to the family's needs. My father was hopeful. I was not. In truth, I did not wish for marriage at that point. I was still young and quite wild at heart. Besides, I enjoyed the attentions of the unmarried men and loathed the thought of hiding beneath veils and travelling by camel to some distant tribe's land.

"Mundhir was the man's name. He was tall and horribly ugly. He was too skinny. His nose was too large for his face and he wore a permanent scowl. Quite unflattering." She reached across the table, absently turning the stirring spoon round in circles as she spoke. "My father greeted them with respect. However, they did not respect my father and thought him beneath them. They made demands of him and set up their tents, which were quite large and beautiful, directly in front of my father's. There was a separate tent for the women and that, too, was quite grand. I was summoned to Mundhir's mother the following morning so that she may appraise me. As if I were a head of cattle!" Anger flared in her eyes and a pink flush crept into her cheeks.

"Not much has changed in that regard, my dear." Luja hoped her words would offer some comfort to the creature but she did not seem to hear them.

"Usaymah was his mother's name. She was a wretched woman. She was cruel to her servants but even more importantly, she was cruel to me." Luja sipped her coffee and tried to fight back the snort of derision that threatened to come out. "I went to her as I was bid and presented myself with grace and a humble spirit. She did not like me on the spot. She kept asking if I was truly a virgin and she hinted that perhaps my father had stolen my maidenhood. I was horrified as the other women stood around Usaymah and laughed. It was humiliating. When I left, I was determined to tell my father that I would not under any circumstances marry Mundhir. I would not, could not, be subjected to the wretched women for my entire life.

"My father had other ideas this time. You see, Usaymah heard how selective I was and that my father wished for wealth. They delivered wealth and a lot more to him. Everything he wanted, they brought him. Silk, camels, livestock, coins… all of it to buy me. I remember the night before everything changed. I went to my father's tent to tell him what I thought. What I found were women in his tent. Whores."

"Oh, dear."

"Yes. They won his acceptance with whores. I cried and screamed at him that I would not marry. He told me that it was done, I would be married the following week, and that I should be a dutiful daughter and thank him for such a prosperous match. Prosperous," Allatu growled. "It was prosperous for him. For me, I was to be the wife of Mundhir, that awful man."

"Did you speak to him at all?"

"Oh, yes." Allatu's laugh was empty of merriment. "I was fetching water the next morning and he found me there at the well. He told me that I would be his wife and he expected that I submit to him." Her face was empty as she remembered the events that changed her life forever. "He held me down and tried to kiss me. I remember his breath smelled of rotten fish. I struggled but he was quite strong. That was the only time in my long life anyone has ever hit me. She reached up and placed a hand on her cheek. "He hit me quite hard and all I could see were bright flashes of light. He managed to pull my dress up and I was exposed. His hands were rough and when his fingers entered me, it hurt."

"My dear, we don't have to continue this part if it is too painful." Luja's heart was betraying her. How could she, a woman, not feel the slightest bit of understanding?

"No, it was long ago," she said picking up the spoon and inspecting it with interest. "He took my maidenhead in the dirt. He left me crying, bleeding, and in pain. I was ruined, you see. I had to marry him then and he knew it. Regardless of any schemes I might have come up with to get out of it, he sealed my fate by force."

"I am so sorry."

"I am not." Allatu met Luja's stare with a fierceness that reminded her that this was not a wounded girl, but something much more powerful. "I cleaned myself up in a stream. I sat by the water for hours thinking of what I should do. I even considered taking my own life. Anything was preferable to marrying that monster. But then, something happened that changed everything."

"I was leaning over the water watching the leaves float by when I saw my reflection. The dried tears and dirt highlighted the colorful bruise on my cheek. But behind me, I saw a woman. I did not hear anyone so I thought perhaps someone had sneaked up on me. When I turned, no one was there. I looked back into the water and there she was again. I could not see her face clearly but she was tall and lovely. Her robes were green— they fluttered in the wind. I remember that." Her face softened as she continued. "I wondered if it was my mother. However, when I called to her, the woman shook her head. The she reached out and placed a hand on my head. This was in the reflection," she reminded Luja. "But I felt her hand. Can you understand? She was there yet she was not."

"Marvelous… " Luja said in awe.

"It was. After she touched me, she was gone, but she left me with something much more than a fond memory by the spring. I was filled with something that drowned the fear and humiliation. She gave me vengeance."

"I see."

Allatu smirked and placed the spoon delicately back on to the table before folding her hands and meeting Luja's stare. "I returned home then. I changed my clothes and wore a veil for the first time in my life. When the night came, I left my tent and made my way to Mundhir. He was sitting beside the fire with his family. I waited. I was ever so patient. I waited until he was alone in his tent. The servants slept outside. He undressed by the light of a candle so the shadows were easy for me to hide in. When he settled down into his bedding, I waited until he was breathing regularly before I moved. Quietly, I stepped closer to him. From inside of my robes, I brought out a knife. It was the knife used for sacrifices and I thought it was quite appropriate.

"I stood over him and watched his chest rise and fall. He slept so peacefully. Even after defiling me as he did, he had no remorse. I knew how to slice the neck of a lamb for slaughter. A man's neck is no different." Allatu watched Luja's measured reaction.

"You killed him?"

"Oh, yes. I reached out and slid the blade across his neck. The red blood bubbled out and then began to spray the room with every beat of his dying heart. His eyes popped open in surprise." She laughed at the memory. "I removed my veil then and smiled at him. He tried to speak but only wet noises came out. He reached for me but had no strength. I stayed and watched as he died. It took a few minutes. Most people believe cutting a man's neck is quick but the dying takes time if they fight it."

"What did you do? Did you run away? Surely his family—"

"His family." Allatu turned and spit on the floor. "After I was sure he was dead, I went to my tent. In the morning, screams and cries from everywhere filled my ears. Alone, I laughed into my pillow. It served him right. It did not take long for his entire family to come storming my father's tent and demand to see me. When he came to me, he was angry. So, so angry… he asked me, *Did you do this thing?* What was I to say? Did I proclaim my innocence or declare myself the victor in a fight for my life?"

"What did you tell them?"

"Nothing. I told them nothing. Perhaps, had I said one way or the other, things would have turned out different. Had I proclaimed innocence, you see, my father would have taken the blame since they were under his protection by law. Had I declared myself the murderer, I would have been killed on the spot. Either way, I was ruined. So, I chose to hold my tongue, for once, and see what the Gods had in store for me.

"Usaymah was standing in the shadow of her son's tent. But when she saw me, she screamed that I was a murderous whore and that I had taken her son to bed, then killed him in his sleep. It was quite the uproar with one part of the camp trying for peace and the other calling for my head. I stood there, head bowed in modesty, and seethed. Usaymah *knew* he had raped me. She knew it and she was angry I got my vengeance on her son. Before everyone, she declared me a murderer and vowed to claim her own vengeance on me."

"I'm starting to see why we currently allow *Allah* to claim vengeance. Humans taking it upon themselves is a nasty business."

"Her vengeance was terrible, Mistress," Allatu whispered. "She and her family went to tend to Mundhir's body. Days went by. We thought they would give him a proper burial in the caves. Father and I certainly thought so. Then, we hoped that they would leave and never return. But it did not happen that way."

"Did you tell your father? Did you tell him the truth?"

"I tried." She reached out or the spoon once more and began twirling it in her hands. "I am not sure if he believed that I did it or not. I was ashamed, you see, to tell him about what happened at the well. I was young and terribly afraid of what it meant for me, not being a virgin anymore. He would hear nothing of it and avoided me. I was heartbroken. Then…" her eyes took on a blank stare as she recounted the rest. "One evening, a few days after Mundhir's death, one of their family servants came to my father's tent. He bade my father bring me to Usaymah so that she may say goodbye and put the unpleasantness behind us.

"My father was more than happy to accept and forced me, rather painfully, to dress and accompany him. The only tent that stood was the large women's tent. Mundhir's had long sense been burned. The others were neatly packed away. I took this as a good sign and followed my father dutifully into the tent.

"Once we were inside, I knew something was terribly wrong. As soon as the servants closed the flap to the tent, four men surrounded us and dragged us bodily before Usaymah and the rest of the family. Normally, a woman was not head of a family under any circumstances. But it was the case with her. She sat on a chair with her daughters and sons around her. She was not wearing her mourning clothes. She wore robes of crimson and a necklace of bones rattled around her neck. I was frightened, as you can imagine. My father demanded of them, 'Let me go! Take your hands off me!' but they tossed him at Usaymah's feet like a dog. Then, without another word, she stood and took a step toward my father. I saw the knife but he did not. He was too busy yelling at the servants who surrounded him. I tried to call out to him… but I heard it. I heard the sound the sharpened knife made when it opened his throat. As he fell backward, he thrashed about, spraying blood everywhere. I cried out to him. He died reaching out to me."

"How terrible."

"It was. She was not finished. Usaymah knelt beside my father and while I watched, cut open his chest and pulled out his heart. I cried thinking she would do the same to me. I suppose underneath all of my fear I was resigned to it, but I was mortal then..."

"My dear—"

Allatu shook her head with her eyes closed. "I must tell it all. No matter the pain."

"Go on."

"She brought my father's dripping heart over to me and smiled. She whispered some words I do not recall, then someone came and brought her a serving dish. The big ones made of bronze... I remember because I was afraid she would eat his heart. The servants grabbed me and dragged me through my father's blood, then tossed me to the ground beside him. I wept. I tried to hold him but they pulled me away. That was when I saw what she was doing—she had thrown my father's heart into the brazier and was chanting while it burned. The tent filled with the smell of burnt flesh and I gagged. Through my vomit and tears, I felt hands on me... oil... I remember it was bitter smelling. Like tar. They ripped my clothes off and continued to cover me in the foul oil. I cried, tried to hide my nudity, but failed.

"I remember some of what she was saying as she brought my father's burnt heart back to me on the platter. Something about balance...

symmetry… above and below." she shook her head and frowned. "I could tell you more about her magic had I paid attention that night. However, I was understandably distraught. I do not understand *how* she did what she did. But I do know *what* she did."

"What did she do, Allatu? I still don't fully understand."

"She took my death. I took her son's life so she took my death. She killed my father as sacrifice for the spell. His heart, when she pulled it from the fire, was blackened and smaller than when she took it out of him. Servants came and brought a statue of a woman in two halves. Inside the statue, she placed my father's heart. Then, they took it to place it near the flames to cook the clay until it hardened."

"No…"

"Yes. That very same statue that you used to call me. You see, that was how she controlled me, My Lady. I was hers after that spell. I do not remember much after they took the statue away. They gave me a drink and forced it down my throat. It burned… it was hotter than whiskey. Hotter than any spirits I have ever tasted since. I do not know what was in it. I do know that it impaired my senses. I could no longer feel my own body. They were chanting and drums were pounding. Then the room was spinning and everything went dark."

Luja sat with her coffee cup in her hand, taking in everything she heard. The girl was poorly treated, if what she said was true. Luja could not even fault her for murdering her would-be husband for his barbaric act. The woman Usaymah scared her. She could only imagine how terrified a young girl would be under the circumstances. How had she gone from that to the monster she was today?

"What is the next thing that you remember? After that night?" Luja asked.

Allatu's face was dark once again. Her eyes took on a feral look that chilled Luja deeply. "I awoke in her tent surrounded by servants. Naked and reeking of the oil they put all over me. I could feel something was different. I wanted to go away but could not force my body to move. Can you understand this?"

"Oh, perhaps better than you imagine, dear. I am an old woman. I know a little something of my body betraying me."

"Yes. That is so. I lay there and waited, thinking it was the drink still having a terrible effect on me. It was not until Usaymah came into view and told me to stand was I able to do so."

"You were her slave."

"Precisely. She laughed when I cried and begged her to let me go. She said she could not and would not release me. I asked her to kill me and she refused. The indignities I suffered at her hands..." Allatu shuddered. "When she said to go, I went. When she said to sit, I sat. When she told me to pleasure her servants, I did. I tried to fight it. I tried so hard." Her hand smacked the table making Luja jump, spilling coffee down the front of her dress. "It was impossible to say no to her. It still is."

Slowly, the realization of what Allatu was saying landed heavily on Luja's soul. "Usaymah, when she died, what happened?"

Allatu met Luja's eyes and both women sat in silence for a moment. "Before she died, she passed me down to her daughter. Then she did the same. Over and over... generations and hundreds of years went by. Then... there was you. You are the heir to Usaymah's curse. I am servant of the blood. Your blood. Now, you know all."

Chapter Nine

What could she possibly say to this poor creature? Luja sat across from a murderous immortal monster and she felt nothing but pity for her. Her ancestor, Usaymah, did not pass down her hatred of the girl. Luja did not want to keep this poor soul captive. She did not want to cause more innocent deaths by having this woman fulfill wild fancies.

"We must put an end to this now, Allatu."

"Certainly, Mistress," Allatu stood and made her way to the door.

"No Allatu… I meant an end to this curse. You cannot want to continue this way, do you?" Allatu slowly turned and faced her mistress with an eerily empty expression.

"What I want has not mattered for a very long time. There are things I enjoy—wine, sex, dancing—but I have not been asked what I want for as long as I can remember."

"Well, I am asking you, now. Do you want me to find a way to release you?"

The immortal woman stood stunned and said nothing. Luja stood and carefully approached her and attempted a smile. "My dear, you did not deserve this. You were innocent."

"I was. I am innocent no longer. Another thing that was taken from me."

"Shall we try? I should like to go to my grave knowing I might meet you in the afterlife, not leave you here for eternity."

Allatu stared hard at Luja in silence. Slowly, Luja watched as her hardened stare became softer and was shocked to see tears fill her large doe eyes. "You are like her. You remind me of Usaymah. Not the terrible parts of her but her strength. You have it."

"Then let us hope I inherited a bit of her magic as well."

After a long pause, Allatu smiled. "Yes. Let us hope."

***

Over the next few days, Allatu and Luja spoke often about the curse and how it could be lifted. Allatu had Luja recount every memory of her grandmother but it was to no avail. Frustrated, they took to writing everything down both of them could remember. In what was once Samir's office, Luja and Allatu sequestered themselves, daily pouring over memories, books, and far too many unknowns.

"There is nothing about the old ways left," Allatu said for the hundredth time as she slammed a book closed. "All this one says is that we're all going to burn for eternity. That is not helpful."

Luja chuckled. "Indeed it is not. But handy when you want people to behave."

Hala took to being Allatu's handmaiden. She brought her wine and cakes from the kitchens, of course, always bringing extra for herself and her grandmother. Her devotion and adoration of the lovely woman was apparent to all, especially to Allatu. She cooed sweet words to Hala, who beamed brightly and happily skipped off to fetch whatever it was that Allatu desired.

The office was in constant disarray. Crumpled papers lay haphazard on the floor and books were stacked into three piles. The first were books they had already scoured and discarded. These Hala would return to their proper place until she bored of the chore. The second were books they were currently reading, trying desperately to find something in old myths or legends to help them solve the mystery. The third were books that would not help them at all. These included many pornographic titles that delighted Allatu when she bored of her own chores.

Around the fourth or fifth day, Samir made his thoughts known about the mess in his office. He came from his bedroom one morning and complained all throughout breakfast. "Why are you using my study? What if I need to meet with important people? Where will I entertain them?"

"Perhaps you should consider the sitting room. That is a pleasant place," Luja said as she nibbled on a piece of fruit. Samir pouted and scowled at everyone. Luja was not concerned with his tantrums. In fact, he had not lashed out at anyone since they arrived at their new home. His wife, however, was ignored completely. Reshma sat in dutiful silence and ate her breakfast. Luja watched her pick at her food with a solemn air about her. Pity filled her heart. She knew Reshma was aware of Samir's many dalliances. He did not work very hard to keep them a secret, either, often coming home in a state of undress and reeking of women's perfume.

The older children occupied themselves with school work and the swimming pool. Daayna had made friends with a few other girls and they spent many hours giggling and talking about whatever it was young girls enjoyed. Aadil was a very busy boy and finally far happier than Luja had ever seen him. All in all, the children were doing well. The adults were the ones who suffered.

The new kitchen staff was far happier to be employed by the family. This pleased Luja to no end. Allatu, though, seemed restless. Luja would not allow her to grant any wishes or make anything easier on anyone. "If I am not useful to you, Mistress, what will become of me?" Allatu begged again as they made their way to the study.

"You are useful, dear. You know how to read many languages and we must continue our search."

They carried on, sending Arman out in search of specific books the house library did not have. Eventually, he softened toward Allatu, much to her pleasure. It started when she read to them the hieroglyphs from an Egyptian book of the dead. Arman was fascinated and asked Allatu to read more. As Luja watched with a smirk, Allatu and Arman huddled together pouring over ancient Egyptian texts.

Allatu was quite happy to read whatever he asked of her. Never having been in love before or even regarded as a person, she became even more beautiful, if that were possible. She began to watch for Arman every morning and greet him at the door. One morning, Arman brought Allatu flowers and Luja watched as they smiled at one another the way young lovers do. She wished Allatu could be happy and live a full life. She wondered more than once that, if she was able to break the curse, would Allatu live through it? Would she be able to live a normal life? Would she die?

Those thoughts and more kept her up at night. The guilt she tried hard to suppress. However, alone in her rooms, she often thought of Zaabit and his mute family. Mute because Allatu cut their throats in their beds. She would take the weight of their deaths to her grave and beg their forgiveness in the next life. Luja did not want these burdens, but they were hers. A woman has many burdens, but speaks of only a few. That was something her mother told her long ago and Luja found that to be terribly, and sadly, true.

The following evening, Luja and Allatu met in the study to continue their search. It surprised them both when the door opened and Arman stood in the doorway. Behind him was Samir.

"Whatever is the matter, Arman?" Allatu asked. Indeed, Arman looked frantic. His face was flushed and Luja noticed the front of his shirt was torn.

"What is it?" Luja demanded. However, Samir stormed into the room dragging a crying Hala behind him. "Let the child go."

"She is my child, Mother." Samir slurred. He was noticeably drunk, standing in the office that was supposed to be his, swaying side to side while his youngest child tried to release his grip on her arm.

"You… how dare you? I am man of this house and I… ouch! Stop that!" Hala was kicking his shins and fighting heroically. Allatu stepped forward and tried to take Hala's arm. Samir yanked her painfully away and pointed his finger at Allatu. "This is your fault… you demon whore!" Hala let loose another kick that sent her father hopping on one foot. Allatu once again tried to grab Hala but Samir fell sideways taking her with him.

As soon as Samir hit the ground, Arman jumped on top of him in a gallant effort to restrain his rage. Hala scrambled from beneath the men crying as she reached for her grandmother. Samir reached out, grabbed one of her small ankles, and pulled her just as she stood, causing the little girl to hit the floor painfully.

"Stop this! Stop this at once!" Luja cried but no one listened. The men were cursing at one another and Hala was crying like a banshee.

"Mistress, shall I? Allatu asked. Luja nodded. She wanted her little Hala safe and then she wanted to throttle her drunken son.

Allatu approached the two wrestling men and gave Samir's head a sharp kick. He screamed violently but stopped grappling with Arman to cradle his head in his hands. Arman scooted back on his rear end and reached up to take the hand Allatu offered him. Luja cradled Hala in her arms and Allatu held Arman's hand. All of them waited to see what Samir would do next.

"Hala, dear one, I want you to go run along to your mother. Can you do that?" Hala nodded and headed toward the door. Before she could reach it, Samir was back on his feet like a panther and snatched her back. Hala wailed for her grandmother and even for Allatu to help her.

"Now, Samir, you need to let the girl go. You are hurting Hala," Allatu said calmly. Luja knew her calm was only skin-deep and the immortal woman was concocting several ways to hurt Samir.

"You... you said anything I wanted," he slurred his words and shook Hala like a ragdoll. "I said I needed a plane... I need to fly. Why is that so hard to do? Why has my dear mother," he swayed drunkenly and looked at Luja. "Why has Mother decided to stop giving us what we need? Does she want things to go back to how they were? Does she want to humiliate me? Does she not love her son?"

"That's preposterous—"

"Pre... preposterous, is it? My little daughter here," he shook Hala until her knees gave out and she slumped against his leg. "She tells me you two are trying to release Allatu. The demon whore wants free, does she?" His laughter drowned out Hala's cries.

"I'm sorry Grandmother... so sorry..." Hala wailed.

"Samir, can we leave these ladies alone and maybe have a drink together? I could use another." Arman said ruefully. Luja nodded her approval, silently appreciating Arman's quick thinking.

"No! No more drinking tonight for me or for you." In one unusually graceful move, Samir let Hala go, reached into his waistband, and produced a black pistol that he turned on the group. "You have been helping them, Arman," he sneered. "You think I am stupid. A stupid man who does not know what is happening in his own house! I will not let you. She is mine!"

"I am not," Allatu cut in. Samir stared at her confused for a few moments and then smiled.

"You are if I say you are."

"I belong to the women of this family. Mistress Luja owns me. You do not."

"I see. You're all in this together." He waved the pistol around, making everyone flinch except for Allatu. Hala crawled toward her grandmother, tears streaming down her face. Luja reached out for her but the sound of the gun cocking chilled her to her soul.

"Don't do that, Samir." Arman said, taking a step toward him with his hands raised. "She's just a little girl. Let her go so we can all talk about this."

Samir did not say a word. He simply turned toward Arman, pointed the gun at his chest and fired a deafening shot. All three women covered their ears in reflex. Hala screamed and Allatu stared as her lover fell to the floor, eyes wide with shock. A bright red stain grew on his shirt as he settled on the floor.

"Bastard," Samir growled. Allatu knelt beside Arman, hands fluttering over his wound. "He's dead... dead... dead...dead. He was a son-of-a-bitch." Samir laughed a little as he stumbled forward. "Give me my daughter," Samir said and he pulled Hala up by her hair.

"Papa!" she screamed.

"Samir, no!" Luja cried.

"Don't worry, you can have her back," he stepped away from his youngest child, pointed the gun at her back and smiled. "Tell the whore to give me what I want and the girl will go free. Deny me and she dies." He laughed a little then continued. "Don't worry, I have two other daughters. No one will miss this one." Hala cried, her screams tearing Luja's heart. Surely her mother heard what was happening. Maybe she was calling for help?

Luja knew Samir did not have much time. Allatu placed a kiss on Arman's brow and stood, her lover's blood on her hands, and glared at Samir with death in her eyes.

"Stop this at once. Your daughter is hurt. You've scared her. Please, my son, I know you are a good man. Do not hurt Hala."

"Do not hurt Hala," he mimicked. "You do not tell me what to do anymore, Mother. Give me what I want now."

Luja looked to Allatu and then into the eyes of her beloved granddaughter. It looked as though the girl was praying and that broke Luja's heart to pieces.

"Do not give in to him, Mistress." Allatu's voice was hollow but firm. I warned you the night we met that this man would be your ruin. Do you remember?"

"What?" Samir tried to stand still but the booze had him shifting his weight from side to side and struggling to focus.

"I remember."

"I said he should die then. I do not regret those words for I see that I was right after all."

"Ha! You can't kill me, demon whore. My mother would never allow it. And, as you two keep saying, you have to obey her. What kind of a mother would she be if she told you to kill me?" he laughed again and Luja saw the gun drop a little. "Mothers love their children," he went on. "Parents will do whatever they have to keep their children from harm, right, Mother?" He looked to his mother and she saw nothing of the little boy she once knew.

This monster standing before her, holding a gun to his own child after shooting another man so thoughtlessly was not her son. "Mother, you tell your demon whore to give me what I want. It's only fair, Mother, unless you want to say goodbye to Hala tonight? I'll make it a fair trade, her life for my wishes. I think that's a balanced offer if you ask me." Luja only halfway listened to his ramblings. A dreadful and alarming thought had taken hold in her mind and she tried to recall what Allatu told her of the night her death was taken from her. *Balance. Symmetry. Above and below.*

"Of course..." she said to herself. Allatu turned her head sharply to her mistress with a question in her eyes. Luja held up her hand to Allatu telling her to be patient. "Samir," Luja said as she stood and took a step forward. As she did, Allatu mirrored her movements from the other side. "Samir, I have something to say."

He swayed and attempted to focus on his mother. "Something to say? You have something to say? Well, let's hear it, Mother."

"Before I do, Hala needs to leave the room. I will not have her here any longer. I shall have Allatu escort her out if I must." Luja said, calling on all of her strength to move forward toward the ending she knew had to be.

"Fine. Get out of here, little Hala." He said.

Allatu motioned for the girl to come and Hala threw herself into her protector's arms, crying. Luja stepped forward to make sure the girl was able to leave. Allatu was whispering in her ear as Hala nodded her head. Then, they were alone. Luja, Samir, Allatu, and the dead Arman.

Without taking her eyes off her son, Luja spoke to Allatu. "Is she gone?"

"Yes, Mistress."

"'Yes, Mistress.'" he mimicked. "Now, say what you will, Mother. I have things to do once you give me Allatu back."

The women stood shoulder to shoulder staring at the drunken man before them. "I will not be giving Allatu back to you, Samir." His head jerked up, anger in his eyes. "You are my son. Once my sweet boy with light in his eyes. But that boy is gone. I see that now. You have done horrible things. You treat your wife like a servant. You ignore your children. You have sex with whoever is willing to spread her legs for you. You killed a man tonight. You threatened to kill your own daughter."

"I did not hurt her… only a few scratches. She'll heal," he slurred.

"Allatu, once, a very long time ago, a woman did not hold her son accountable for his actions. Instead, something was taken from you. Many things were taken from you actually, but one thing in particular."

"Yes," Allatu said, watching both Samir and Luja carefully.

"I can't give him back to you," Samir said, pointing to Arman's body. Then he collapsed into a fit of giggles.

"No. He is already dead. But you and Allatu are alive."

"Mistress—"

"I can end this all and I will." Luja bent over and held her son's face in her hands. "I love you, my boy." Then she placed a kiss on his forehead. She stood and sighed heavily. "Allatu, dear one, do you still want it?"

Allatu let out a strangled cry as tears fell from her sad eyes. "Yes. But—"

"No 'but', Allatu. I'm afraid we don't know what will happen when it's done. I don't know if you will survive or not."

"When what's done?" Samir asked but he was ignored.

"I want to go, Mistress. I want to be with Arman if I can."

Luja nodded. The room stood still. She heard her heartbeat in her ears as she spoke to Allatu. "Allatu, I give you my son's life for your death. May his passing release you from your bonds of servitude forever."

"Yes, Mistress," Allatu said. "Thank you."

Luja could not watch. She might have been strong enough to give the order but she was not strong enough to witness another death by her command. She walked from the room as Allatu reached for Samir's throat. He gave a strangled cry but Luja closed the door behind her, crying softly against the frame.

Her ancestor, Usaymah, spoke of balance the night she took Allatu's death. Luja realized that only someone from her family could undo the curse only if the price was equal to that which was taken.

Balance.

It had to be her son who died to give Allatu the rest she deserved.

Symmetry.

In death, everyone was forgiven, or so she was told. Luja hoped they would all be waiting for her when she finally left this world. She would forgive her ancestors. She would forgive her son.

Above and Below.

Epilogue

Luja watched as the dirt fell over her son's grave. She remembered sending the servants in to the study to see if they needed anything and then hearing them scream. From that moment on, the house was in chaos.

Reshma cried and mourned her dead husband, although Luja suspected Reshma was not as torn up as she appeared. The two eldest girls mourned their father properly but devoted their time to taking care of their mother. Hala stood stoically beside her grandmother without saying a word. Her quiet watchfulness told Luja her youngest granddaughter understood more about these events than she believed at first. They did not discuss it. By mutual silent agreement, the two stayed very quiet and let everyone mourn around them.

The day before they put Samir in the ground, they buried Allatu. Luja had sent servants to their old home to dig up the golden statue. Only she knew what was inside and she thought the statue should be buried with the girl. A piece of her family to go to the afterlife with her, Luja thought as the white shrouded body disappeared underneath piles of dirt. In the dead girl's hands, Luja placed a curved blade with a beautiful gold hilt. Only she and Hala were in attendance for that funeral.

Arman's body was sent back to his family with the tragic news of his death. Luja prayed he and Allatu were finally together and waiting for her on the other side.

Aadil took his father's passing hard. He could not understand what happened to him. In fact, no one understood why he decided to kill his two most trusted confidants and then himself. That was the story going around anyway. Luja was happy to let that be what everyone thought.

Only she knew that her son's heart was torn from his body and set on fire. Only she knew the beautiful exotic woman called Allatu was found dead, covered in blood of both men, but with no sign of injury anywhere on her body.

Luja would take these and all of the rest of her secrets to the grave. As she walked to the family car, Luja held Hala's hand and gave it a squeeze. Hala would inherit these secrets as well. Together, they would survive. She would make certain of it. They were family, after all.

Bound by secrets. Bound by blood.

Turn the page for a special preview of
Mel Massey's novel

Earth's Magick

Book One

~Earth~

Available now from Solstice Publishing

Chapter 1

Mela Malone spent a lot of time wondering if she was dying. While other twenty-two year old women worried about what to wear, whom to date or made wedding plans, Mela worried about how she would survive.

It started as nightmares that were dark and horrific. In the beginning, she couldn't remember details and spent the better part of the day recovering from the lack of sleep. As the days wore on, her health began to decline and the nightmares got worse. Many times over the past few weeks, people commented on how tired she looked. Her boss constantly tried to get her to go to the doctor. Mela knew that this couldn't go on indefinitely, so this trip out of town was a desperate attempt to save her life and find some answers. If there were hope, she would find it tucked away in an old bookstore, the only shop that catered to the occult within fifty miles of Mela's hometown. If what she was looking for was there it would be worth the long journey.

Mela knew when she arrived that she would find the help she needed. She smiled as the thick smoke from the burning sage wrapped around her. The wooden floors creaked beneath her feet as instinct guided her to the far side of the room.

She lightly ran her hand along the rows of books as she walked down the aisle. Mela searched for one book in particular. It didn't take long to find it because she knew which one she came to buy. They had shown it to her. They had shown her this bookstore as well. She had no idea who *they* were but *they* helped her. The Four.

They only came to her in her dreams - the good dreams that were too few. Each one of The Four came dressed in different colored tunics. One wore brown and another wore a dark blue. She couldn't remember much else except that they spoke with her in the dreams. Many of the details were lost somewhere between the world of dreams and her painful reality, except for flashes of images. They would stand, towering over her, and point to the sky. They would guide her down a dark road and talk to her as they walked.

Other times, they stood looking at her as a ring of fire surrounded them. However, she could never remember what they said. She did recall that they showed her a book. She remembered smiling as she held it in the dream and when she awoke, she knew what they wanted her to do. In her heart, she believed The Four had come to help her rid herself of whatever it was that was trying to kill her. Flashes of the hideous Old Woman that haunted her dreams snaked their way into her mind and she shook her head to force the anxiety that rose with the image.

After scanning each book she passed, Mela found the familiar green cover and pulled it from the shelf. The weight was even familiar to her. Having always been a lover of books, she ran her hand across it and felt the smooth green surface. No letters desecrated the flawless leather.

She hugged it tightly to her chest and closed her eyes. It was something real and tangible to connect her to the vivid dreams. She had understood this right, at least.

Mela took the book to the cashier who eyed her strangely when she paid for it. Mela endured concerned looks from most people when they saw her lately.

Mela felt placing her beloved book in a plastic bag wasn't quite respectful enough, so she no-thank-you'd the sales lady and carried her new purchase out of the store.

As odd as it seemed, there was an immediate friendship with the book in her arms. It radiated warmth and promised to help, teach, and protect her now that they were together. Of course, this could all be in her imagination, but she felt relieved on the drive home; believing it to be true. She felt better prepared for whatever might happen next too. She kept reaching over to it just to feel the comfort it brought her. Comfort wasn't something she had experienced in weeks.

The attacks had begun to have very real physical effects. She had never been extraordinarily beautiful but she was considered pretty. However recently her brown hair was dull and her normally sun kissed skin was pale. The dark circles under her eyes scared her. She looked and felt like she was fading away.

Her best friend, Wyatt, in his colorful and flamboyant way, made her see the need for action. She smiled and shook her head as she remembered his reaction when he saw her after she had tried to hide her deteriorating state. She couldn't hide anything from Wyatt for long.

He brought her dinner, takeout of course,

and almost dropped the food on the doorstep when she opened the door. She remembered seeing that his beautiful hazel eyes went wide with fear. Hell, she was concerned for herself. Not sleeping and slowly dying will do that to a girl.

When he forced her to reveal the truth, Mela had broken down in tears. She was sure, positively, that she was going crazy. However, upon hearing the story, Wyatt proved to her what a dear friend she had. He held her; assured her she wasn't crazy (any more than normal) and they made a plan of action.

They decided that she would follow the clue to the bookstore and see if the book existed. Even though Wyatt seemed skeptical, she knew she would find it and she did. What scared her the most was that she had been right. That meant that everything else was real too.

He was waiting for her at her house when she drove down the long driveway. As she gathered the book in her arms, she felt the sultry southern heat wash over her. It was only ten in the morning and it was already suffocating outside. Summertime in south Texas is not for the weak.

Wyatt opened the door for her and her German shepherd, Bear, greeted her with a wagging tail and wet nose. She ran her hand through his coarse hair and let out a heavy sigh. Wyatt ushered her to the table in the kitchen and settled himself beside her. Her cat, Kat, jumped on the table to investigate what everyone was doing. Wyatt quickly picked him up, scratched him behind the ears and placed him back on the floor.

They stared at the book. For a moment, Mela was afraid. To decide to open this book, to accept the help The Four had given her, would change everything she thought she knew to be real. An air of anticipation hung around her as she looked at the book. It was the dark green of summer and the leather was supple. How could such a beautiful thing be bad? Regardless of how shaken she was, the desperate need for help overrode whatever reservations she had.

She batted away doubts as images from last night filled her mind. As she slept, her bed had filled with scorpions. Real live scorpions - stingers and claws included. She could still feel the tickle of their tiny, armored legs as they crawled on her. As they marched their way up her legs, she screamed in terror as the old woman held her down.

It was Bear who had been her savior. He leapt at the woman and, though she disappeared moments before his teeth snapped closed, Bear had made her go. Mela was sure of it. The scorpions were another story. Wyatt had gallantly charged into Mela's room brandishing a baseball bat, ready to fight. However, when he saw her bed crawling with scorpions, he had run, screaming, faster than Mela could. She was certain that that was the last time he would volunteer to stay the night as her bodyguard.

His hand on her shoulder brought her back from the visions of the previous night. She reached for the book and slid it closer to her. Mela's hands shook slightly as she lifted the cover.

What had felt like an air of expectation before, now sat like a heavy fog over her as she opened the book. Sitting next to her, Bear let out a whine to let them know that he too felt the gravity of the moment. The cover was thick and heavy and the paper looked worn and aged. Wyatt's sharp intake of breathe as a subtle blue light shined for a moment from the pages of the book mingled with her gasp of surprise.

She saw strange symbols scattered on the first page. Then, slowly at first, the symbols moved. Sliding across the paper they bent and reformed until they spelled out words she could read:

The Elementai will summon the Spirit.
So he is, the Elementai will be.
And as the Elementai is, so he will be.
One the master, the other the student.
In the darkness they will find the light.
In the light they will find the darkness.
Seek what is hidden for evil to be thwarted,
Forgive the darkest parts of all.
The Elementai will reunite.
So mote it be.

About the author

Mel Massey is a native Texan but has called California, Florida, Missouri, and Washington home. Mel went to college in California and studied Cultural Anthropology where her field of study had a huge impact on the creation of the Earth's Magick series. Mel is also politically active and a (sometimes loud) supporter for equal rights, non-GMO products, and animal rights

Mel can be found tweeting nonsense or having hilarious discussions with readers on Facebook. Occasionally, she leaves those particular vices and writes about magick, witches, monsters and all the lovely dark things lurking in the shadows.

Visit her website at www.melmassey.com

Visit www.solsticepublishing.com for more titles
like this one.